BOOKS BY S. M. BOYCE

The Grimoire Saga

Lichgates

Treason

Heritage

Illusion

The Misanthrope

The First Vagabond: Rise of a Hero

The First Vagabond: Fall of a Legend

The Demon

The Fairhaven Chronicles

Glow

Shimmer

Ember

Nightfall

Standalone Novels

Ari

STAY CONNECTED

Boyce posts official artwork, updates, and random things that will make you laugh on Facebook, Instagram, and Twitter.

Boyce also created a special Facebook group specifically for readers like you to come together and share their lives and interests, especially regarding the Grimoire Saga novels. Please check it out and join in whenever you get the chance! Everyone in there is amazing, and you'll fit right in.

https://www.facebook.com/groups/Grimoire-Readers/

Sign up for email alerts of new releases AND exclusive access to the Grimoire Saga Fandom Encyclopedia: the official guide to Ourea exclusively for the Grimoire Saga's biggest fans. The encyclopedia is

ONLY available to Boyce's VIP email tribe, so sign up now to get access:

https://smboyce.com/email-signup-pages/grimoire-saga/

Enjoying the series? Awesome! Help others discover the Grimoire Saga by leaving a review at Amazon: **http://mybook.to/first-vagabond**

THE FIRST VAGABOND: RISE OF A HERO

BOOK SIX OF THE GRIMOIRE SAGA

S. M. BOYCE

BOOK DESCRIPTION

Ourean legends of the First Vagabond have survived a thousand years, blossoming in pubs and alleys even as the great Bloods of Ourea tried to squelch his name. But the myths glorify the deeds and forget the man he was—Cedric, a boy from a small Hillsidian farming village.

As a young man, Cedric discovers a terrifying defect in his nature. He has no blood loyalty, which means he can defy his king—something that has never happened in recorded history. But what begins as a flaw evolves into a strength. Citizens begin to listen to Cedric, and he discovers that if he leads, others will follow.

But there's a catch. The more who follow him, the

more famous he becomes. And the more famous he becomes, the more targets he finds pinned to his back.

He's a wanted man. A traitor. And as Cedric begins to embrace the title he's been given — the Vagabond, the only man alive with no master — he ignites a revolution. After all, no one has defied a Blood and lived to tell the tale. No one, that is, but Cedric.

CONTENTS

For Mom
You're a brilliant, guiding light, and I love you.

CHAPTER ONE

AGE 9

Mid-Summer

Endervere, Kingdom of Hillside

The forest glowed green in the noon rays of a hot, summer sun. A bead of sweat dripped down Cedric's face while the canopy above him rustled with a breeze that hadn't reached him yet. The dappled shadows from the sun through the tree-tops above danced along the forest floor, casting light gray spots across his arm. The tendrils of a weeping willow drifted lazily, and the foggy warmth of the forest clung to Cedric like tiny weights along his skin.

He wiped his brow, squinting as he rummaged through the underbrush, looking for a purple leaf with blue veins. A leaf brushed his ankle. He scratched the exposed skin, his pants too short since May, but he'd been told he wouldn't get new ones until autumn. Apparently, he grew too much, too quickly.

Exhausted and thirsty, Cedric plopped down in a bed of clover to rest. His neck ached from hunching in his hunt for a leaf he was fast beginning to suspect didn't exist. It wouldn't be the first time he'd been sent on a fool's errand—and he doubted it would be the last. A bird sang in the tree above him and, as he leaned on his hands to drink in the day, something tickled his hand.

A great, red beetle trekked across his fingers. He studied the bug, recognizing the black streaks across its back as a wanderer beetle. Harmless, sometimes crushed into a powder and used for dye. He grimaced, imagining the poor thing writhing as it was flattened into powder, and he set it in the grass.

Laying on his stomach, chin on his hands, he kicked his feet in the air and smiled as the beetle ambled away into an emerald-green bush. A flash of purple within the brambles caught his eye. He sat up straighter, grinning, and summoned his magic. Tension pulled on his shoulders, slowing him down, but he didn't care. With a flick of his wrist, the branches curled away to reveal what hid within.

An ivy vine. Purple leaves. Blue veins.

"Stone, I found it!" Cedric shouted.

A young man with a mop of black hair and a thin beard lining his mouth peeked out from behind a white tree about fifteen feet away, dark red stains on the sleeves of his white tunic. The thin man nodded curtly. "Good, good. About time, boy. Let's get started."

Cedric pouted. He'd been at this for twenty minutes, but he still thought he'd found it pretty quickly. Nothing he did ever seemed to be fast or good enough for Stone. Cedric shoved his hands in his pockets and kicked the dirt with his toe, shuffling as he waited for the man to finish up whatever he was doing and join him by the vine.

Dead twigs snapped as Stone neared, and Cedric tried to shake himself from his sadness. The last time he had pouted, Stone made him clean the entire house from top to bottom, scrubbing the wood to get it clean. He'd gotten more than a fair share splinters, and he had no intention of scrubbing anything else for quite some time. Even if all he wanted was a *thank you*, Cedric would have to pretend he was fine.

As Stone neared, the enchanting scent of lilac and pine spread through the clearing. The blend was the mark of an isen, the natural scent of a powerful creature that could steal souls and live for centuries.

Stone knelt beside him. "If you remember nothing else from our lessons, Cedric, remember this: everything is energy."

Cedric nodded as if he understood what it meant. It was something Stone said all the time, every day, as if the more he said it, the more it would make sense.

Didn't matter. It was still nonsense.

Stone gestured toward the purple leaf and the vine it sprouted from. "Take this plant, for example. It survives off energy, and it only grows here, in this particular location. Nowhere else in Ourea. Do you know why?"

Cedric shook his head.

"Because of this." Stone pushed himself to his feet and gestured to the weeping willow. With a sweeping gesture, he pulled back the curtain of branches to reveal the base of the trunk. One of the roots had grown out of the dirt and stretched upward toward the canopy, creating a low archway as its thinning tip leaned against the trunk.

And yet, the archway showed another world.

Though Cedric should have seen the forest behind the tree, the portal revealed a cliff overlooking an ocean. The sun burned along the horizon, orange and pink as candy. The diluted colors reminded him of watered-down ink on a stained canvas.

"A lichgate," Cedric said under his breath. A portal to another part of Ourea, to a landscape he had never seen.

Stone nodded. "A well-hidden one, too. Observe." He pulled an oval gemstone from his pocket, a milky-white rock Cedric often saw used in Stone's experiments. As the young man neared the lichgate, the milky white stone glowed brilliant blue, brighter than the purest water Cedric had ever seen.

"Interesting," Cedric said, copying the way Stone tapped on his jaw whenever deep in thought. "The stone glows green for the lichgate by our house."

"Very good. You're right. Everything is energy—you, me, this lichgate—but we all vibrate at different levels. Lichgates are no different than us, the animals, or the yakona. Now walk through and take this." Stone offered him the glowing blue rock, and Cedric took it.

In Cedric's hand, the rock filling his palm faded from blue to green. The brilliant hue would always remind Cedric of home—it was the same color as the lichgate leading into their house. As he neared the lichgate, the stone again faded into a beautiful shade of blue.

Wait a minute...

He hesitated, eyeing Stone's empty hand. The rock was always white as milk when Stone held it, as well as any time he left it on the table or stowed it away. It was naturally white, so why did it turn green for him?

Stone gestured to the lichgate. "Well? What are you waiting for?"

Cedric eyed his mentor, the question on the tip of his tongue, but his instinct told him to wait. To be silent.

To behave.

He swallowed hard and shook his head. "Never mind."

Cedric ducked through the archway, preparing himself for the unpleasant but altogether harmless act of walking through a lichgate. As he stepped through, his gut churned, like something had punched him in his stomach. A wave of nausea rose in the back of his throat. His cheeks flushed. A flash of blue light sparked in his periphery.

And yet, as soon as it had hit him, the nausea passed. His stomach settling, he stood a little taller.

Wind roared by him like a stampede he couldn't see. Its salty bite stung his nose. He squinted, trying to get his bearings as the sunlight blinded him. He stood on the edge of the cliff he had seen through the archway, the ocean crashing like thunder below. Brilliant blue water, an orange sky, the sunset reflected in pink ripples along the waves—the vivid colors sang to him, no longer diluted by the lichgate.

In his hand, the rock still glowed with the same brilliant, blue hue as it had in the forest.

He glanced over his shoulder, wondering what to do next, but Stone gestured for him to return. Cedric obliged. After another kick to his gut and another flash of blue light, he was once more in the forest.

"The color didn't change," Cedric said.

Stone nodded. "Every pair of lichgates operates at the same energy level. That's how they connect, that's how the magic knows where to send you when you walk through it."

"What if we changed it? What if three lichgates had the same energy?"

Stone nodded. "Good questions. I don't know yet. It's one of the mysteries of magic, and I intend to dissect it."

Cedric shuddered on impulse, consumed with a sudden sense of dread he didn't fully understand. He thought of the beetle being crushed into powder, of the bug losing its life for something as trivial as a colorful shirt.

He pushed away the thought.

The shouting of boys arguing filled the air, followed by laughter. Footsteps thundered along the deer trail hidden by a thick row of bushes, and Cedric caught a glimpse of several blonde heads bouncing through gaps in the underbrush.

Stone grimaced. "What the devil possessed them to come all the way out here?"

Cedric shrugged, leaning toward the ruckus with the desire to chase and join in whatever game had started. The kids from the village didn't usually come out this far, and their voices tempted him to run along and join in the fun.

He rarely got to have any fun.

"You are not joining them, Cedric," Stone said, as if reading his mind.

"Why not? Their fathers let them play instead of working. Why won't you let me?" His voice had a higher pitch than he'd intended, whiny and with an extra layer of annoyance, but he didn't care. He always did what he was told, and it never seemed to make Stone any prouder of him.

"First of all, I'm not your father. We've been over this. You may call me your mentor."

Cedric kicked the dirt, refusing to look at his so-called mentor. Stone fed him, cared for him, clothed him. He certainly *acted* like a father... most of the time, anyway. It was as close as Cedric had ever come to one.

Stone wagged his finger. "And, second of all, you can't play with them because you'll likely get hurt. Boys roughhouse, they bleed, and no one can see you bleed. We've been over this one hundred times."

"But why? I'm like them, aren't I? Why can't I have friends?"

Stone pinched the brow of his nose and sucked in a deep breath, like he often did when an experiment failed, or he couldn't find the mushrooms he wanted for a potion. "I don't care if you have friends, even if I don't understand the appeal. But you can't be seen bleeding. I've made that very clear. You bleed red. They don't."

"Why? What's wrong with me?" Cedric rubbed his forearm, a knot in his throat. He wanted to cry, to scream with frustration, but Stone never rewarded emotion. Cedric did his best to stay calm, to be as level-headed as his not-father.

Stone tapped his finger on his jaw, eyes wandering the forest for a moment before he answered. "You're simply different. You're something better."

"But I'm a yakona, aren't I? Same as them?"

Stone hesitated, watching Cedric the same way he watched his experiments—cautiously, detached from the outcome, as if waiting for it to explode.

"Of course, you're a yakona," Stone eventually said. "What else could you be?"

CHAPTER TWO

AGE 17

Mid-Summer

Endervere, Kingdom of Hillside

Cedric woke to a silent house.

Usually, the scream of the teakettle on the fire served as his cue to get out of bed. Stone never knocked on his door, but a chair scraping over the floor, dishes rattling—these signs of life indicated he needed to be awake, present, and downstairs within minutes.

But today—nothing.

A gust blasted by outside, his small home creaking in the gale. It blew through his open window, ruffling his hair and shooting a grateful chill over his skin. He stood, wiping sweat from his brow as he stretched. A bird whistled, the song fading as it passed his room.

He yawned, rubbing his eyes as he left his small room and trotted down the narrow stairs. The house Stone had built before he was born barely had room for the two of them, but it was the only home Cedric had ever known. It would suffice.

Still groggy, he stumbled past the dining table and armchair, into the tiny kitchen. A fire burned in the red-brick fireplace, though the inch-high flames barely crackled. Cedric pulled a log from the dwindling pile in the corner and tossed it on the fire, shooting ashes into the air.

Empty.

Cedric crossed his arms, eyes wandering over the oak hutch by the kitchen door, one of the house's three exits. He swore there were more doors than walls in this place, but Stone had built the house around two lichgates, incorporating them into doors that led to other parts of Ourea.

The question was where had Stone gone off to this time?

With a groan, Cedric returned to his room to change. Stone had left again in the middle of the night. It happened about once a year, never at the same time, and always meant Cedric needed to feed and occupy himself, sometimes for months at a time.

He tugged on his shirt and the worn pants that were just a little too short from yet another recent growth spurt. The brown patch stitched into the knee had a few stitches loose, but he would have to see these out until they were unbearable. It bothered Cedric to wear clothes that didn't fit, but Stone didn't seem to see the benefit in wasting money on such frivolous things.

Cedric grimaced. His stomach rumbled.

He trudged to the door, determined to make the most of his not-father's disappearance. With a grumble and a muffled curse, Cedric threw open the only door that wasn't a lichgate and charged into the daylight.

His worn boots stomping along a dirt trail, Cedric made his way toward the nearby village, Endervere. Tree trunks whizzed by, nothing but brown blurs as he hurried, another hunger pang snaking through him. Since he was six, he'd taken this route each time Stone left. It led to a perfect house on the edge of Endervere, with its tended vegetable gardens and the kindly old couple who lived in it. When they'd first found him, ravenous and with bruises all over his arms, they'd force-fed him bacon and apples. They'd held him, told him stories, laughed with him.

They'd been everything Stone wasn't.

And yet, when Stone came for him in the middle of the night, Cedric had obliged. He always returned, even though, to this day, he didn't understand why.

He kicked a rock, and it sailed into the underbrush. A bush shivered as the rock made contact, and Cedric shoved his hands in his pockets. He wanted a family, a sense of support and love. Instead, he had… whatever it was Stone did.

Stone wasn't a father, but he wasn't a very good mentor, either. Whatever Stone was to him, Cedric knew for certain the isen was one thing: strange as all hell.

"So that father of yours is gone again, is he?" Marian pursed her lips and set a plate of steamed cabbage leaves and two slabs of red meat on the table. Cedric's mouth watered, and he nearly grabbed the beef with his hands. Marian liked to smack his shoulders when his manners weren't to her liking, though, and he restrained himself. With another rumble of his stomach, he took the cutlery lying on the table and dug in.

"Yes, he's been gone since last night," Cedric said between bites. It was easier to lie, even though he hated doing it. This village was part of the kingdom called Hillside, a group of yakona who made sport of killing isen like Stone. If they knew what he was, he would be murdered on the spot, and Cedric didn't hate his not-father enough to get the man killed.

A tickle of worry burned in the back of his mind, resurfacing an old fear he tried so hard to bury: if

Cedric wasn't Stone son, he had to be one of Stone's experiments. He wasn't sure which would be worse.

Miriam patted his shoulder and tended the fire, rolling up her sleeves as she fanned the flames. She wiped her brow, and Cedric again noticed the sprawling tattoo along her arm. He'd seen the whole thing once—it trailed from her wrist to her shoulder, an intricate web of vines that matched the one on her husband Adam's arm as well.

Lifelines. They marked a union of two souls for life: the bond. The couple would always know where the other was, if they were in danger. All yakona had them.

Everyone except Cedric.

He absently rubbed his shoulder. He'd rolled his sleeve up to his elbow but, despite the heat, he didn't dare roll it up farther. Any yakona who hadn't yet experienced the bond had shorter lifelines down to the elbow. He'd noticed on some of the street brawlers when they ripped off their shirts for a duel. Thus, Cedric always had to wear long sleeves rolled no higher than his elbows, even in the worst summer heat. Sweat and discomfort were a far cry better than the stares and murmurs he would get in town as a yakona with no lifeline.

He paused, mind wandering as the worrying thought came again: Stone must have done something to him. He had no proof except that he didn't belong. He bled red while the Hillsidian yakona bled green. He had no lifeline while every yakona he'd met did, each of their natural tattoos as varied and beautiful as the last. Even babies were born with them.

Lifelines were, yet, another reminder of Cedric's abnormality. His oddness. His wrongness.

Adam cleared his throat, the massive man tapping a sausage of a finger on the table. "You'll be rid of your lousy father soon, boy. You're nearly a man, after all, about ready to go out and live life on your own. Ever thought about what you'll do? You have options. Farming. Fighting. Even exploring. The capital has been recruiting new isen hunters, after all."

"I'm not really a fighter." Cedric resisted the impulse to grimace. Even in their small village on the outskirts of the Hillsidian domain, they couldn't escape the capital's culture. Isen hunters were revered, celebrities who stole the attention and hearts of the Hillsidian people for doing what so many feared to do. Many young men craved the wealth and fame a career as an isen hunter would bring.

But isen stole souls, and it was deadly business. Many disappeared, and rumor had it there was always an opening in the capital's isen hunter academy.

Marian set a glass of water by Cedric's plate and sat in the chair beside him. "I would rather you didn't get caught up in all that mess anyway. Become a farmer, do some good for the village. There's some unclaimed land just south of here, and you could supply us with some much-needed variety from what the Avery family manages to produce. I'm sick of cabbages, truth be told. With as many strapping young men and budding families as we have in this town, we could use another farm."

Cedric nodded and sipped his water, but he had no idea of what would come next. Many young men left their families at eighteen, but his was no ordinary family. Stone could hardly be called family at all.

"Speaking of strapping, young men and budding families, we expect grandchildren," Adam added, waggling his finger.

On reflex, Cedric spit out his water, managing to turn his head toward the floor at the last second. Adam and Marion roared with laughter, and the old man slapped his hand on the table.

"It's a little early to be thinking about that," Cedric said, but he couldn't stifle his laugh. He often wondered if this was what it was like to have parents, people who loved him, who cared for him. He had so often thought about staying, of living his life with them instead of the man who so fervently insisted that Cedric was something other, something separate.

But Cedric wasn't an isen. He didn't have the barb in his palm like Stone did, and if he was an unawoken isen—isen who hadn't yet faced Death to get their abilities—Stone had never completed the ceremony. He didn't have isen scent, either. No, Cedric was certain he was a yakona, albeit a broken one.

His smile fell, and something clicked in the back of his mind. Fear. Fear drove him back to Stone, the only one alive who could understand his being different. He bled red—what would Marian and Adam do if they found out? Kind as they were, he'd never tested their loyalty. He'd never pushed, or dared to dream, they would accept him for who—for what—he was.

He suddenly understood what always drove him back to the grumpy, old isen deep in the forest, in a house hidden between two lichgates. With the realization, he lost his appetite. However, not wanting to offend Marian or have to answer questions about his sudden mood, he begrudgingly bit into what remained of the meat on his plate.

"Don't worry, my boy. We could always ..." Adam paused, his attention turning to the window by the front door. Smile fading, brows scrunched with worry, he stood.

"What's wrong?" Cedric glanced out the window but saw only the dirt road running past the front door.

"Oh, my word," Marian said under her breath. She held her hand to her chest and got to her feet, her tiny slippers scuffling over the floor as she hurried out the door. Adam followed.

Cedric stood, concerned. He ambled after the old

couple. As he emerged, a young woman opened the door of the house beside theirs. She lifted a child in her arms, her blond hair loose around her shoulders as she walked along the street, eyes focused on the road ahead. Another family from farther down the road—a man and his three raven-haired daughters—walked together, hand in hand, eyes all trained on the road that led into town. Young and old, they wandered out as if in a daze.

Confused and a little frightened, Cedric nudged Adam. "What is going on?"

An exasperated expression crossed the old man's face, a strange combination of irritation and bewilderment. It said, *are you out of your mind?*

Cedric almost pressed the issue. He'd never seen anything like this, and not a bit of it made sense. They walked as if they were sheep, led by a herding dog he couldn't see, and no one would tell him what was going on.

Silence settled over the procession. A gust blew the trees around the path, the clattering of leaves like a round of applause, but the forest was still. Nothing twittered. Nothing sang. Nothing scampered.

Enough.

Cedric tugged on Miriam's sleeve and grabbed Adam's arm, pulling them back to the house. They leaned toward him, but each shook him off without looking back. He tried again, tempted to drag them along if he had to, but he didn't want to make a scene.

He tensed, concerned for them, tempted but unable to tear them away from whatever was happening.

The path bent to the left, dozens of dazed heads following along blindly. More villagers joined as they neared town, stepping onto the wide path from smaller trails and the doorsteps Cedric passed. Caught up in the tide of bodies, Cedric tightened his hands into fists as he prepared himself for whatever awaited beyond the bend in the road.

The butcher's building appeared. A street lamp after that. Mostly, Cedric could see only the heads of a crowd. It was as if the entire village congregated in their tiny town square. Nothing seemed worthy of the blind march into town, nothing that would justify—

A flash of emerald green fabric with gold trim caught his eye. A helmet. A spear.

An army.

Soldiers with green tunics and the golden tree of Hillside embroidered on their chests stood along the edge of the crowd, their eyes ahead as they saluted. Golden helmets covered their heads, polished and perfect. Cedric gaped at the nearest one, mind racing for an explanation. The guard's eyes darted to his and narrowed as their gazes locked. A shiver raced along Cedric's skin, and he quickly looked away.

The crowd pushed him forward, toward the statue of their Blood, Tristan. The king's effigy stood on a pedestal in the town square, the centerpiece a daily reminder of who ruled them. Cedric had studied its features before—the square jaw, the militant, short hair, the beard, the cold, unfeeling eyes.

Blood Tristan was said to rule more as a general than a king. He waged war with the other yakona kingdoms, often taking and torturing prisoners himself for information on the other kingdoms' whereabouts. He'd massacred villages, hunted isen himself in his youth. His stealth was the stuff of legends—apparently, he could snap a man's neck without the man knowing. The rumors of the way he dismembered enemies on the battlefield, casting their blood across the ground, always made Cedric grateful the man was miles away.

And yet, the Blood now stood on the platform beside the statue of himself.

Cedric gulped, terrified. This was bad. Very, very bad. Dread shot clear to his toes. Blood Tristan was royalty, a man who had led wars and lived in finer comfort than anyone in this town would ever know. He had no reason to be here unless something truly important had led him to the sleepy village. Something like an isen, perhaps, or the experiment he was raising as a son.

Cedric had to get out of here.

Blood Tristan raised his hand for silence, despite the lack of conversation. Hundreds of chins lifted to watch him. His gold cape fluttered in a breeze, the popped collar brushing his neck. Green embroidery along his spotless, white tunic reminded Cedric of the milk-white rock Stone carried in his lichgate experiments.

The Blood gestured to the crowd. "Every man between sixteen and twenty-five, come forward."

Heads bobbed in the crowd as men obeyed. One boy to Cedric's left, a redhead around his age with pale freckles, flinched as if he had been slapped. The boy hesitated, back arching as if a fishing line were pulling on his shirt, forcing him to obey. He took slow steps, but he eventually made his way forward.

Cedric, however, didn't move. Tall enough to be noticed, he didn't have much time. His eyes darted around, desperate for an escape. Guards blocked the road he'd used to enter town, and other soldiers blocked the rest of the nearby streets. He ducked, scanning the edges of the crowd for weak points until, finally, he spotted an unattended alleyway between two houses. The twenty feet between him and his escape was closely packed with villagers, but Cedric made his way toward it, hoping they were too involved with their blank stares to notice his direction.

"I'm disappointed," the Blood said, his voice thundering through the town square. "We asked for recruits to help us in our plight against the isen, and not one person from this village volunteered. Not one. You force me to set an example, to show that this war with the isen requires sacrifice from us all."

Cedric's heart raced. His feet shuffled a little faster. Ten feet left before he could duck into the alley and run as fast as his feet could carry him back to the forest. He could find the trail from there, and so help him, he would never return to this village. His dream of a loving family aside, the risk would be too great.

Five feet. So close. The breath caught in his throat.

"You!" the Blood shouted.

Cedric's heart skipped a terrified beat. He'd been caught. His mouth ran dry. Trembling, horrified, unable to breathe, he tilted his head to catch the Blood's eye.

But instead of eyeing him with an evil glare, the Blood pointed to the young boy who'd been standing next to Cedric, whose shoulders shook as he stood at the front of the crowds, now under the royal man's scrutiny.

"Yes, your Majesty?" The boy's voice squeaked.

"What is your profession?"

"I help my father with his farm."

No time. Cedric had to use this distraction to his advantage. He resumed his escape, careful to keep his head low.

Almost there.

Cedric could barely contain his panic. He longed to race forward, to run into the alley and propel himself and the forest, but he couldn't let himself be seen. Had to be cautious, despite the way his hands shook. Slow and steady, despite his tendency to bump into the very villagers he was trying to slip away from. His very life now depended on the stealth he had failed to acquire.

"Are you an only son?" The Blood asked the boy in the town square.

"Yes."

"You're dismissed," the Blood said, turning to the next young man. But as he shifted, his eyes lifted and met Cedric's.

No. Oh, *Bloods*, no.

Cedric's heart soared into his throat. He'd been discovered.

In the fleeting second when their gazes met, a look of utter confusion passed across the Blood's face. It was as if he couldn't fathom the thought that Cedric had disobeyed, that he wasn't already in the group of boys gathered under the statue.

"Bring that one to me," the Blood ordered, pointing at Cedric.

Cedric bolted, pushing past a young woman as he raced into the alley. It didn't matter if the entire army chased after him, he had to escape. He had pushed his luck, taking too much of a risk, and he had failed. He should've known better than to mingle with the yakona who hunted isen for sport when the man who'd raised him was an isen himself. Cedric had craved company, family, and his desires had undone him.

Guards pushed through the crowds, yelling for him

to stop. He didn't. Metal clanked. His throat burned. He ran, pulse racing, fueled by fear.

A soldier ran into the alley after him, and another appeared ahead of him from between two houses. They both drew their swords, and Cedric skidded to a halt. He glanced wildly around, desperate for another way out, but the only remaining alley had two guards blocking it. Trapped, he summoned his magic. Tension pooled in his shoulders, but he wasn't alone—every yakona could use magic, and if these were royal guards, they were the best of the best.

He didn't stand a chance against soldiers strong enough to protect the Blood himself, but he would try anyway.

Pain splintered through his arm as he summoned fire from his palm and threw it, the blaze arching toward the soldier between him and freedom. The man lifted his hand, and water materialized from the air, extinguishing Cedric's flame with a hiss.

The man charged.

Stone had always said knowledge was useless unless it could be used, but Cedric had never been in a fight before. He didn't know what to do. Fueled by instinct and panic—and completely out of ideas—Cedric threw another fireball. It missed, singing the dirt instead of the guard's face. He aimed again, but a hand grabbed his raised arm. Someone kicked his leg. He fell to his knees, grimacing as agony shot through his body from the blow. Something sharp bit into his wrists, the cold metal like ice on his hot skin. He cursed under his breath as pain shot up his forearms and into his elbows.

"How did you disobey me?" The quiet but deadly voice came from behind him.

A hand pushed against Cedric's head, keeping his gaze on the ground. Within seconds, polished black boots with barely a speck of dust on them came into view, and Cedric felt the weight of an angry gaze on his shoulders.

Someone grabbed his hair and pulled, lifting his head until Cedric caught the gaze of the Blood. The royal man grimaced, nose wrinkling, as if disgusted by Cedric's presence.

Blood Tristan sniffed and narrowed his eyes. "You smell that?"

The soldier next to him, who had a gold medal on his chest, shook his head. "What is it, your Majesty?"

"Hyacinth," the king said, as if it were a damning piece of evidence.

Another shot of dread nearly froze Cedric's heart. To him, it *was* damming evidence. Hyacinth was the flower they used to mask Stone's isen scent on the rare occasions he came into town. It had worked for decades, but apparently this Blood was a better isen Hunter than any Stone had run across before.

The Blood set his thumb and pointer finger on his

forehead, his eyes narrowing as he stared at Cedric. For a moment, Cedric had no idea what was happening. It seemed as though the man had a headache, or was debating someth—

Pain ripped through Cedric's body. He screamed. It tore him apart from inside, as if his muscles were being peeled off his bones. He couldn't see. He couldn't think. He could feel only the agony. It consumed him. It raged on, lasting forever, until Cedric thought this was the end. It burrowed within him until he became convinced he would never feel the sun again, never smile again, never have hope again in his life.

Eventually, the pain mercifully stopped. He collapsed, the soldiers no longer holding him in place. Dirt filled his mouth and stuck to his tongue as he gasped for air, for anything to sooth the lingering ache in his bones. Tears pricked his eyes.

A rough hand grabbed his arms again and yanked him to his knees. His head lolled, rolling on his neck as he struggled to hold himself upright.

"Fascinating," the Blood said quietly.

On impulse, Cedric cursed as loud as he could. He had a brief pang of regret afterward, seeing as this man could easily kill him, but he couldn't think straight. "What the hell did you do to me?"

One of the guards grabbed his hair in punishment and lifted his head to face the royal man standing before him.

The Blood set his hands behind his back. "If you'd been an isen, that technique would've exposed you for what you are. But it did nothing. You disobeyed a direct order from me, and thus you have no blood loyalty like the rest of your villagers. Yet you are not an isen. You're not a—hmm."

"I'm not a what?" Terror swam like ice through Cedric's veins.

Blood Tristan shook his head, eyes narrowing. His voice softened, almost impossible to hear. "You can't be. No, I don't know what you are. It's fascinating."

"I haven't done anything wrong. This is no way to treat one of your subjectsTo him, it was damning evidence.," Cedric said, his voice shaking. The soldier's grip on his hair tightened in punishment.

"I'm fairly certain you're not one of my subjects," the Blood said with a deep frown. He lifted his gaze to the soldier beside him. "Throw this boy in the cage. We'll deal with him back at the capital."

A mighty tug on his bound hands lifted Cedric to his feet. Shaking from whatever the Blood had done to him, he could barely walk. They pushed him forward, and it was all Cedric could do not to yell for Stone—for anyone—to help him.

In his heart, he knew no one would come. As the soldiers dragged him through the alley, Cedric became certain of one thing.

He would die.

CHAPTER THREE

AGE 17

Mid-Summer

The Kingdom of Hillside

Several days later, Cedric sat in the corner of a stone cell with an iron gate for a door. The sliver of a window near the ceiling offered his only light. He sat on a bed of dirty straw, staring at his hands as he tried desperately to think of a way out of this mess.

Spikes along the inside of the cuffs bit into his wrists, stinging with every movement. Groggy, unable to think straight, he tried again to summon flames for warmth. Tension pooled along his back as it always did when he used magic, but pain splintered from the spikes in his skin. He suspected they had poison of some kind on them, blocking his magic.

Marvelous. Slouching, he settled against the cold stone wall of his prison.

A stomach pang shot through him, and he doubled over on impulse. At this point, he'd eat a rat if he could only find one. He'd barely eaten. They fed him stale bread a few times, but nothing else. On the ride to Hillside, he'd been thrown in a dark box, unable to see a thing during the entire trip. He hadn't even known the time of day. The days since had blurred together, and he hadn't had a moment of rational thought.

During meals, the soldiers took his cuffs off. Slivers of clear thinking would return in those moments, but he was never left alone, and they always put the cuffs back on too soon.

Cedric had to escape. He needed a plan.

But he couldn't think of one to save his life.

Blood loyalty. It wasn't a term he had heard before, but he wasn't a fool. Everyone had obeyed a silent command to leave their homes, to come to the town square. The boy next to Cedric hadn't wanted to walk forward when called; quite the contrary, it almost seemed like he had been pulled forward. Forced by some uncontrollable impulse to obey. None of them had a lick of free will. Whatever hold the Blood had on them, he controlled them completely.

And Cedric was immune.

He stared at his hands, wondering yet again what he really was. He was no isen, as the Blood himself had proven. But for the first time, he was beginning to wonder if he was truly a yakona, either.

So, what am I?

He shook his head. No. He could not think about this right now. He had to focus on a way to survive because he suspected he wouldn't have much longer. He'd likely been left alive because he was nothing more than a novelty. A curiosity. Possibly a threat to the Blood, whose power came from controlling the masses.

Cedric would have to be clever, or he was going to die.

"Did you enjoy the trip?" A quiet voice asked. The tone carried a deadly warning in it, almost a gleeful triumph.

The Blood stepped into view in the hallway, the thick bars of the iron door revealing only slivers of the man's face. Without the gleam of golden helmets behind him, it seemed as though the Blood had come alone. It likely didn't matter. The Blood's broad shoulders and barrel chest reminded Cedric of the warriors he'd read about in Stone's books. The man could probably kill Cedric himself without even drawing the sword around his waist.

"The trip was lovely," Cedric said dryly.

The briefest of smirks passed across the Blood's face before the already familiar frown returned. "Not an isen. Not a human. Probably not a yakona. What are you, boy?"

Cedric's ear twitched at the familiar word. *Human.* According to a lecture he'd heard once from Stone, humans were creatures from beyond the lichgates, a race that looked like Hillsidians but lacked their magic and stealth. They never came into Ourea and likely didn't even know it existed. Frankly, most yakona didn't know they existed, either.

Yet, Blood Tristan did.

The king knew too much. It grated on Cedric's nerves. "How do you know about humans?"

"We're isen hunters, boy. It's the Hillsidian way, and those vermin live everywhere. They've run into the human world to escape us, and we followed. I've seen more than you've even dreamed of."

Cedric crossed his arms, his grip on his elbow tightening until his nails nearly broke skin. He couldn't let the Blood see his terror, but his heart raced. At any moment, the execution call could come. He had to play his cards wisely.

The Blood leaned against the gate, shoulder resting against the bar as he examined Cedric. "I've decided to study you. My scientists will examine you, and you will comply with their every request, no matter what it is. No matter how much it hurts. No matter how much they ask of you. Do you understand?"

"And if I comply, will I be allowed to return home?"

Blood Tristan studied him for a moment. His cold

eyes reminded Cedric of a predator observing its prey: silent and still. "You will never return home."

This was it. Death. The Blood intended to dissect him, to deconstruct him until he made sense, and then dispose of whatever remained. Cedric had seen Stone do this with animals before, and a part of him had always wondered if his mentor did this to living creatures, to yakona and perhaps his fellow isen as well. Blood Tristan certainly wasn't opposed to it.

Panic burst through the dam of self restraint in Cedric's core, flooding his body and urging him to run away. But he couldn't. He was trapped, so he said the first thing that came to mind. "If you kill me, you'll lose valuable insights into our world that could help you in your war against the isen and against our fellow yakona. I can help you. I'm valuable. But if you kill me, if you dissect me, you'll lose it all."

Blood Tristan frowned, eyes narrowing in suspicion. "Explain."

Cedric's throat ran dry, but this was a victory, however hollow. Armed with only his wit and the lessons he'd learned from Stone's books, he had the king's attention. Now all he had to do was tempt him with the one thing any military commander wanted: advantage.

The only problem? Cedric knew almost nothing about the kingdom's inner workings or what the Blood actually needed. He racked his brain, trying to think of anything from Stone's endless lectures that could help him here.

Nothing. He panicked. His mind raced, and he did his best to stifle the urge to fidget under the king's glare.

Well—there was one possibility, but it was a stretch. Stone had once mentioned the Hillsidian kingdom was hidden by heavily guarded lichgates, but that wasn't much to go on.

No choice. Cedric ran with it.

He cleared his throat. "I know lichgates and the inner workings of magic. My," he hesitated, having trouble finding a word for Stone in his terror, "my father and I study magic in all its forms. We've mastered lichgates, especially, you see, and—"

"Get to the point."

Cedric sucked in a quick breath to calm himself. He'd been rambling. He couldn't waste this man's time. Every word had to count. "However strong your army is, your city isn't protected if it can be found. Let me lock the lichgates you use to access your kingdom, and no isen or encroaching army will ever find you. You'll be completely protected."

If this interested the Blood, the royal man didn't let it show. He still frowned, the same small wrinkles around the edges of his mouth. He didn't move. He simply watched Cedric, as if waiting for him to crack under the sheer pressure of his gaze. Though tempting,

Cedric maintained eye contact, swallowing hard in his attempt to keep a level head and resist the impulse to beg for his life.

The Blood stood, hands behind his back. "How long will this take?"

Cedric's knees shook from the stress of negotiating for his life. Grateful he was sitting, he leaned on them to hide it. "I'm not certain. I'll need to see your lich-gates first."

"Convenient."

"It's complicated magic," Cedric said, adding a shrug to feign confidence in himself.

Blood Tristan looked off into the hall, eyes shifting out of focus. "I will allow you to try. If you fail, you will be studied. I will have my men find your father, as it seems he has interesting information for me as well."

"Oh, t-t-that's not necessary," Cedric stuttered, hands trembling. Blood Tristan had smelled the hyacinth; he had no doubt he would be able to detect Stone's isen nature instantly. Stone's presence in the capital would jeopardize them both.

The Blood grinned, the sneer lighting up his face as he left. "Oh, I believe it's absolutely necessary. You'll be shown to a room shortly."

Cedric stood, desperate to say anything to change the Blood's mind. His thoughts raced, but he couldn't come up with anything.

Blood Tristan paused, hands once more behind his

back, and returned his heavy gaze to Cedric. "I warn you, boy, against disappointing me. Don't try anything devious. Do what you're told when you're ordered to do it, and I might let you live. Understood?"

His mouth dry, terror seeping to his knees, Cedric simply nodded. He was out of clever things to say, out of bargaining chips, out of ideas. As the king disappeared into the hallway without so much as a footstep to give him away, Cedric sank again to the floor, terrified of what would happen the moment Blood Tristan realized Stone was an isen. Terrified, he could admit, of what would happen to not just himself, but to Stone as well.

Whether or not Cedric was an experiment, some failed attempt to understand magic, Stone was the closest thing Cedric had ever known to a father. He was family, albeit a broken one. And yet, Cedric's stupid mistake would get them both killed.

CHAPTER FOUR

AGE 17

Mid-Summer
The Kingdom of Hillside

T he sun had nearly set before guards came to take Cedric away. He spent the walk through the dark corridors debating if it was a trick, if one of the soldiers would run him through with their spear or lead him into a crazy, old man's office to be studied. But after an agonizingly long walk, they opened a little, wooden door and then shoved him inside.

At least they'd taken off the cuffs.

His new bedroom had only a bed and a chamber pot in one corner. Its lone window featured iron bars and a narrow view of the stables. Exhausted and ready to sleep, he sat on the mattress. As he collapsed on the lumpy thing, a clump of hay shot out of a hole in the corner of the bed and onto the floor, but he didn't care. A scratchy mattress was better than dissection.

One hand in his hair, he stared at the floor, eyes out of focus as he fought to come up with any kind of idea as to how to survive his new predicament. He'd promised to do something he'd never even tried for the most powerful man in all of Hillside. Now, he had to deliver.

He collapsed on the bed, cursing himself.

A smattering of ideas burned through his brain, and he grasped at each with the hope it would offer him a way out. Blast through the door with a bolt of lightning —he'd get attacked, maybe killed by the guard. Attack a guard the next time one came in—again, he'd lose against these hulking soldiers. Somehow break through the bars on the window—fall to his death, likely. The drop looked far.

He groaned.

Cedric had gotten this far by luck, but his luck could change in a heartbeat. There were no doubt soldiers headed back to his home village to look for Stone and finding him would mean disaster for them both. If Blood Tristan had somehow figured out hyacinth flowers could mask the scent of isen, there would be no way for Stone to hide what he was. They would discover him. They would kill him.

Though Stone had always insisted he wasn't a

father, the thought of losing him shook Cedric to his core. Tears pushed against the corners of his eyes, and he sniffled. The old isen was as close to family as Cedric had ever come.

Cedric felt trapped. If they caught Stone, they were done for. If they didn't, Blood Tristan would still expect him to deliver on his promise. His lie. He said he could change the lichgates, but he'd only ever watched Stone do it twice. He had neither the tools nor the knowledge to do it himself.

If Stone abandoned him, Cedric would die here. He rubbed his face, terrified and desperate for a solution.

Something thumped gently against the wooden door, and the brass knob jiggled. He studied the entry, the only way in or out of his tiny room and tensed. He balled his hands into fists, mind racing as he debated what this could be: perhaps the Blood had sent a quiet assassin to do away with him, regardless of his promises; or perhaps word had spread already about his lack of a blood loyalty, and a vigilante had come to rid the world of someone so broken as him.

He swallowed hard.

The door cracked open, and a thin form slipped in, her green skirts twirling as she pivoted and quickly shut the door. She leaned her back against the entry and held a finger to her lips, shushing him. Her beautiful face caught him off guard. His fear faded, and he paused for a moment to marvel at her. About his age.

Thick, black hair curling past her shoulders. Milk-chocolate skin. Large, dark eyes with long lashes. Heart-shaped face, and full lips twisted into a smile. She held a book in one hand, though Cedric couldn't read the title. Her emerald green dress offered a stunning contrast to her smooth skin, and the scent of roses wafted from her like perfume.

Cedric's fear of death shifted into a fear he would say something stupid to scare her off. Maybe she had the wrong room.

She bit her lip, grinning mischievously. "You're Cedric, the boy from Endervere, aren't you?"

His mouth parted in shock. "You know who I am?"

She giggled. "Everyone in the castle's talking about you. The Hillsidian with no blood loyalty! I had to see for myself."

Ah.

He stared at the divots those poisoned spikes had left in his wrists. "Come to see the freak?"

A small gasp escaped her. She reached for him but stopped short of touching him. "I'm so sorry. Cedric, no, that's not what I meant at all. You're not a freak. You're amazing."

Baffled, he once more studied her. It must have been a joke at his expense, but she didn't laugh. Her smile had disappeared, and she instead watched him with furrowed brows and a soft frown.

He quirked an eyebrow. "Amazing?"

She wrung her hands, eyes wide. "I'm not supposed to be here. I'm not supposed to be talking to you, no one is."

"Then how did you get in?"

"I have friends in the guard." She gestured to the door.

Ah. Cedric rubbed his tongue over his back molar, debating his options. Maybe he could get her to use her connections and let him out.

She smiled, continuing. "I had to cash in a favor, and I only get a few minutes, but I had to—well, perhaps this is stupid. After all, I don't know who you are, and I don't know if you'll tell Blood Tristan that I came. I can only ask that you keep this between us. I will be severely punished if anyone discovers I came to you. I want to tell you there are those of us who think you're gifted. You're a vagabond, a man with no master, and we envy you, Cedric."

At first, Cedric didn't know what to say. Stone had broken him. There was nothing to be envied, nothing to amaze. And yet, this beautiful young woman had come to him in the middle of the night, and from the sound of it, risking her life to simply talk to him.

It didn't make sense.

Warning bells went off in Cedric's mind. This could be a trap, some kind of trick or spy from the Blood to prey on him, to discover his weaknesses and get him to reveal something incriminating. As much as he wanted to trust this girl, he had no idea who she was. He couldn't trust anyone, not here.

Not yet.

"I'm sorry," she said. "I got so excited, and I just barged in when you've had a hard day. I haven't even introduced myself yet. My name's Helen."

"It's a pleasure to meet you, Helen," he said, his manners overwhelming his common sense for a moment.

She smiled again, this one a little more strained than the first, and offered him the book in her hand. "Rumor is Blood Tristan wants to keep you here for a few days to break your spirit. I didn't want that to happen, so I thought I should bring you something to read. A guard told me you impressed the Blood with your knowledge on lichgates and magic, so I figured this one might entertain you."

"Thank you." He took the tome, running a finger over the embossed title. *A History of Hillsidian Kings.*

"I thought it might help to know who you're dealing with," Helen added softly.

Despite his doubts, Cedric smiled, grateful. "This is very kind of you, Helen."

Her smile broadened, and her shoulders relaxed. "If you want anything else just ask. I work in the royal library, so I can bring them to you one at a time without getting caught. But—and this is important, Cedric—you absolutely must hide it if a guard comes in. I'm friends with some of them, but not all of them. They, well, they ..."

"They what?" he pressed, a pang of dread shooting through him.

She forced a smile. "Let's just say some of them are more loyal to Blood Tristan than others. It's hard to tell who will be on duty outside your room at any given time, so just be careful. They don't knock."

Cedric nodded, grateful for the warning and smiling for the first time in days as he ran his thumb along the binding of the book she'd smuggled out of a library for him.

She watched him for a moment with a soft expression he'd never seen before. Her eyes crinkled, the barest smile on her lips. As quickly as she had come, she retreated without a word, the door clicking softly behind her.

In the silence that followed, Cedric sat on the edge of the bed with the book in his lap, wondering if he could trust this beautiful girl. In his heart, he wanted to call her back, to finally have some good company after all the death threats and close calls. The voice of reason deep in the back of his mind—a voice that had over the years developed to sound just like Stone—warned him not to trust anyone. Connections could be corrupted, trust could be broken, and those he relied on could betray him. The only way to live a safe life was to separate himself from those who could deceive him.

He stared at the door long after she'd gone, wondering if it was worth the risk to at least try.

CHAPTER FIVE

AGE 17

Mid-Summer
The Kingdom of Hillside

For several days, Cedric wasn't allowed to leave his room. No guards entered. No summons from the Blood. Just him, his book, and the chatter of the military who passed beneath his window on the way to the stables. He couldn't make out conversation, just the hum of voices and the occasional laugh.

He spent most of his time slumped against the wall, rump firmly planted on the itchy bed. Only the books Helen brought in the dead of night kept him company, and he was pretty certain he would have begged to be let free if not for her. She never stayed more than a few moments, though she had begun to stay a minute or two more each time. She had come for him every night so far, always with another book and sometimes with a bit of food—a loaf of bread or some dried meat when she could find it.

In the mid-morning on day four, Cedric lay on the floor, staring at the ceiling as he chewed on the last bit of the jerky she had brought him, eyes out of focus as he replayed her laugh in his mind. She had shared a story with him about Blood Tristan's son, a spoiled ten-year-old with a grotesque appetite, getting his head stuck in a bucket during sword training. Both he and Helen had to cover their mounts to stifle the laughter and keep their voices down.

He smiled again at the memory, wishing she were here with him.

Stone's voice in the back of his head warned him again—no connections, no dependence, not here. It wasn't safe or wise to trust anyone in this castle, no matter how kind, or smart, or funny, or beautiful—

The door swung open, smacking against the wall with a thundering bang.

On impulse, Cedric shoved the last of the food in his mouth to hide it. He swallowed without chewing, cursing the lump in his throat as he tried to force the food down. Despite the panic, a wave of gratitude flushed through him that he had stowed his latest book from Helen under the mattress already.

A soldier stood in the doorway, his massive frame

blocking nearly the entire exit. His green uniform had the same gold insignia on it as Cedric had seen on the guards in his home village. A sword hung around the man's waist, and he scowled, his square face twisted with anger or annoyance. Cedric couldn't quite tell. The man had a scar over his left eye, and the lid drooped a bit.

Helen hadn't been kidding. These guards didn't knock.

"The Blood has summoned you," the guard said, his voice deep and scratchy.

Cedric gulped. The memory of sitting in a cell, barely able to concentrate due to the poison in his body, flashed in his mind. Blood Tristan thrived off control, dominating those around him. Panicking, Cedric wondered which of his two, terrible choices was about to play out: Blood Tristan either found and discovered Stone, or he didn't. Cedric would either be killed on the spot or expected to perform magic well beyond his capabilities.

He stood, hands shaking. "What does he want?"

The guard sighed as if it were a stupid question and grabbed Cedric by the arm. The burly man pinned his wrist behind him and pushed him against the wall. Pain shot down Cedric's arms. He grunted, doing his best to comply and not cause a scene.

But the guard pulled out a pair of spiked cuffs.

Cedric tensed, shying away from what he knew

would come next: nausea, lightheadedness, weakness. Pain. So much pain. He eyed the door, weighing his options. He could distract the guard, run, hope for the best ...

... or he could let this happen, and hope the Blood was in a good mood today.

Both options relied too heavily on hope and luck for Cedric's taste. If he ran, he would be caught. He didn't know this castle. He didn't even know how to get out of it, much less where to go from there.

He had to play along, at least for now.

The spiked cuffs bit into his skin, and he gritted his teeth to suppress the sting. His head spun a little, but it was nothing compared to what would happen if he were to wear the cuffs for more than twenty minutes. He hoped this meeting would be quick.

The guard marched down the hallway, and the ache in Cedric's wrists distracted him from the castle layout. He tried to focus on the wooden doors, to memorize the route they were taking, but there were too many turns, too many identical sconces lighting the way, too many hallways that looked exactly the same.

The soldier led him around a corner and into a hallway lined on one side with open windows. Brilliant, white daylight streamed through. In the sunbeams, specks of dust hovered, suspended in the air. Cedric squinted, the light almost too much to bear. As they passed, Cedric caught the fleeting glimpse of trees and a rope bridge slung between two of them.

As the guard led him down a flight of stairs, Cedric's muddy mind raced with what would happen when he spoke to the Blood. He didn't know if the deal would change, if the Blood would dissect him after all. If his wit had failed him. A pang of dread burst through him, made worse by the fear that, perhaps, they had discovered Helen's visits. Her stolen books. If, perhaps, she hadn't been as stealthy as she'd thought. He wondered if she would be there in chains beside him— or worse, smirking as the Blood revealed it was his plan all along to break Cedric's will. To prove Stone right.

Snap out of it, he chided himself. This way of thinking wouldn't serve him. He shook his head, suppressing his fears with a terrified sigh. It is all speculation fueled by panic, and he had to go in with his wits about him. The spikes in his wrist shifted, shooting pain down his arms. He stumbled. The guard yanked on his arm, driving more shooting bursts of pain through Cedric's arms. He squeezed his eyes shut, gritting his teeth in an effort to push through the agony.

The soldier stopped short. Cedric bumped against the bulky man as he threw open a door to reveal a large study. More brilliant sunlight exploded through two floor-to-ceiling windows across the room. Books filled shelves on every wall. A desk sat between Cedric and the windows, nothing more than a silhouette in the blinding glare until his eyes began to adjust. A figure shifted in a tall chair behind the desk, blurry and nothing but shadow until he spoke.

"Have you thought of anything else you need to tell me?" The familiar voice sent shivers down Cedric's spine.

Blood Tristan.

Cedric's eyes finally adjusted. The Blood glared at him, still as a statue. Beside Blood Tristan, a young boy sat in an ornate chair, his legs kicking and unable to touch the floor. The seat dwarfed him, its red and gold detail nearly swallowing the boy. He couldn't have been more than ten years old, but he folded his hands in his lap as if he were a judge and tilted his chin ever so slightly upward, looking down at Cedric despite his shorter stature. Though curious as to why a child would be in this meeting, he had a far greater concern.

The door slammed behind him, and he tilted his head just far enough to look out of the corner of his eye. The guard crossed his arms, blocking the doorway with his massiveness.

Silence followed.

Cedric shifted, eager to get this over with as the spike's poison fogged his mind. This was no doubt a strategy, a way for Blood Tristan to wear down Cedric's defenses and get the answers he wanted.

Cedric debated his options again, but they seemed to be fewer and fewer with each passing moment.

"It seems we cannot locate your father," Blood Tristan finally said.

It took every ounce of Cedric's willpower to hide his relief. He didn't nod or say anything because there was no way to win in this conversation. With Blood Tristan's knowledge of isen, Stone would be discovered immediately and killed on the spot, and the same would likely happen to Cedric simply for associating with an isen and having the gall to call one his father, even if it had been a lie.

Cedric eyed the little boy beside Blood Tristan, recognition blossoming in his mind. Perhaps, this was Blood Tristan's son, the boy who would one day rule the Hillsidian people when his father died. It seemed so odd for a child to witness a meeting with a prisoner. He should be playing. Running around. Dreaming. And yet, he sat as motionless as his father, and with a matching expression of loathing on his tiny face.

As a spike's poison further fogged his mind, Cedric lost control of his wandering thoughts. Memories popped up unbidden even as he tried to focus on the royal man scowling at him across the room. He recalled sitting at the dining room table, smiling as he finished another book—only for Stone to drop one more on the table and snap his fingers. The snapping meant *get to it* or *hurry up* or even *get out of my way* depending on Stone's mood.

Cedric frowned. Since before he could remember, Stone had taught and lectured and commanded instead of letting Cedric play and explore. Neither he nor Blood Tristan's boy were allowed to have childhoods. He couldn't help but wonder if the prince would grow up to be as broken as Cedric.

"Tell me where your father is," Blood Tristan commanded.

"I'm sorry, your Majesty, but I don't know," Cedric said.

The Blood grimaced in disgust. "Don't lie to me."

Cedric leaned forward, brows twisting upward as he tried to prove himself and save his skin. "He disappears, Blood Tristan. It's what he does. I never know when he'll be back, or where he went."

"He simply leaves you alone?"

Cedric nodded. "I wake up never knowing if he'll be there."

The king shook his head. "You lie. No father would do that to his son."

Cedric's lips parted in shock, and the pang of sadness rocked his core. For a moment, he forgot where he was. He forgot the shackles on his wrists. Forgot the massive guard hulking behind him and the boy in the chair next to the king.

He simply remembered the first time he'd awoken

to an empty house and a note on the table. He'd sobbed, only six, and wondered what he had done to make Stone upset with him enough to leave. He'd cleaned the house, organized the books—done every chore he'd ever been given in his short life in the hopes that it would be enough to bring Stone back, to make him worthy of love.

"I see," the Blood said, eyebrow raised in mild curiosity.

Cedric snapped back into the present moment and clamped his mouth shut, confused. "Wh—"

"Your expression told me everything I need to know. Fine, you don't know where he is. We'll monitor your hometown and watch for him. He's a wanted man until further notice. But you, Cedric, made promises to me, and I expect you to see through on them. You will begin working on the lichgates today. Afterward, you will be taken to a new room where you will bathe to make yourself presentable for the next time I speak to you."

Cedric's heart skipped a beat, and he impulsively hoped Helen would be able to find him in his new room.

The Blood continued, leaning on his desk as he pointed a stern finger at Cedric. "This is my offer to you, boy—fortify my kingdom and give me a way to guarantee the isen will be kept out of my home city. In exchange, I will let you live despite your lack of a blood loyalty. There is no negotiation. Do you accept these terms?"

Cedric tensed, jaw squaring as he stood a little straighter, the poison still burning through his mind like a haze. He nodded, more and more willing as the minutes passed to do whatever it took to get these cuffs off him.

"Don't disappoint me," Blood Tristan said.

Cedric nodded again, this time his eyes on the floor. He had no bargaining power here, and even less of a clue on how he would actually deliver on the promises he'd made to one of the most powerful men in Ourea.

As the soldier led him again into the hallway, Cedric's mind raced in panic. He did know how to change a lichgate. He needed Stone and the tools the isen used to work his magic. The best Cedric could do was stall until he found a chance to escape.

His heart sank. What a coward. Disgusted with himself, he racked his brain for everything Stone had ever told him about the lichgates. He needed the milk-white rock, the book of notes Stone kept in his bedroom, and maybe a miracle. Cedric groaned.

If Stone were here, he'd tell Cedric escape was the only option. Yet, Cedric couldn't help but wonder what Helen would say if she discovered he had disappeared in the night, if she would feel as if he had abandoned her. He chided himself—he shouldn't care. He'd only known her for a few days. Still, he hated himself just a little bit more at the thought of leaving her behind.

☙

T rue to the Blood's word, Cedric had been un-cuffed and led to one of the lichgates surrounding Hillside. With seven soldiers surrounding him, Cedric hadn't been given much leeway, but at least the cuffs were off. They'd passed through back alleys, past shopkeepers who averted their eyes and mothers who ushered their children away. A pack of guards around a stranger—it likely meant trouble, and Cedric's dread grew with every step.

Perhaps he could create a diversion when they reached the lichgate and run for his life, escape into the forest and come up with a plan on the way. After all, it wasn't as though he could stay. He'd made a promise he couldn't keep. No matter how this ended, he would make an enemy of the most powerful man in Ourea.

Unless Cedric came up with something clever, he was going to die a very painful death.

His convoy led him to an archway in the trees along the edge of town, similar to the lichgate in the willow back home but with a muted view of a moonlit meadow and surrounded with two dozen frowning men. His grumbling audience watched without a word as Cedric hemmed and hawed, pretending to study the edges of the lichgates as he stalled.

He studied it for what felt like hours, eyes nearly crossing as he stared at the same twig, stroking his chin. After awhile, he stole a glance at the sun.

It had barely moved.

This would take forever. His horrible day simply would not end.

The minutes crawled by, made all the worse by the growing panic in his chest. When the burly soldier from earlier finally gestured for them to leave, it took every ounce of Cedric's self-control to not sigh with relief. The lumbering guard plowed ahead, the six other soldiers surrounding Cedric in a circle, and he followed, head down and hands in his pockets. In his periphery, he scanned the alleys, doing his best to look for an exit.

There wasn't one.

He hung his head with exhaustion and just a hint of shame. There would be no escaping while working on the lichgates. If anything, it would be the time he was most closely watched.

And yet, he had no idea what he was doing.

The cobblestone path became stairs, which became a stone floor. Flickering shadows danced beneath their feet, no doubt from a torchlight. Cedric didn't bother looking up. He continued to scan the halls, to figure out their direction, but nothing looked familiar. The endless passageways all had the same gray walls, the same bare floors, the same sconces.

In time, the soldier in front swung open a door and shoved Cedric through. He stumbled, falling to the hard floor as the door slammed behind him. His wrists hurt. His head ached. He studied his new room. Orange light streamed in through a window on the far wall, iron bars marring his view of an orchard. A bed sat in one corner, a door in the other likely leading to a bathroom of some sort. The Blood had mentioned bathing, after all. He sank onto the bed, the cushion beneath him dipping with his weight. Good. At least he wouldn't have to sleep on straw anymore. His hands wandered over the rough sheets, calluses catching a bit on the cloth as his mind wandered. This was at least an improvement over the chamber pot or a jail cell, but he was still trapped. Still a prisoner.

Someone grunted in the hallway. Footsteps echoed and receded. For good measure, Cedric tried the handle, but it was locked. He leaned his ear against the door, listening for a guard. Someone spoke, followed by a deeper tenor.

Two guards. Lovely. Even if Cedric were to unlock the door—which he'd learned to do as a child to go play with the boys from town—he wouldn't get far.

He cursed under his breath and sank onto the bed, staring at the ceiling as he wondered what to do. He shifted his weight, trying to get comfortable.

Something crinkled, like paper thrown in a bin.

Brow furrowing in confusion, Cedric leaned forward and examined the comforter. The corner of a piece of paper stuck out from under the pillow. When he plucked it out and unfolded it, he recognized the handwriting immediately.

Stone.

Relief swelled through Cedric. At least, of course, until he read the note.

You boneheaded boy—

What the hell have you gotten yourself into? I leave for three days, and suddenly you're a Hillsidian prisoner, and I'm a wanted fugitive? Three days, boy! How do you ruin your life in just three days? Whatever stupid thing you did, you'd best at least pull the lesson from it.

Cedric paused to take a deep breath and steady his rising annoyance. He rubbed his temples, grumbling to himself until he could force himself to continue reading.

On to business.

I've had to shift into one of my Hillsidian souls while I'm here, so you won't be able to recognize me. However, I will be able to communicate with you through the notes we pass in this room. It's surprisingly unguarded when you're not in it.

I'll come up with a plan for your escape. For now, tell me exactly why you were wondering around a lichgate for hours staring at trees. You looked like a fool, but at least everyone here seems to be an idiot. I need to know what they're expecting of you.

—Stone

A pounding headache began in Cedric's temple, and he massaged it as anger boiled in his chest. He couldn't do anything right, not according to Stone.

Time to explain himself, apparently.

He lifted the pillow, hunting for something to write with. Sure enough, a small stick of charcoal lay on the sheets, dark gray smudges already staining the white cloth beneath it.

With Stone's help, Cedric might survive this after all. He grabbed the charcoal and wrote his response in scratched letters underneath Stone's tight script.

Stone—

I have to somehow secure the lichgates and keep isen out, or the Blood will kill me because I have no blood loyalty. He also knows about hyacinth flowers. I don't think the guards can detect the scent as well as he can.

As much as I hate to suggest you steal someone's soul, I think you should become one of the guards so that we can

have conversations while I'm out at the lichgates. I'll need
your advice, and it's the only way for you to go undetected.

—Cedric

He paused before adding one last line.

P. S. Thank you for coming for me.

Cedric set the charcoal and note between his bed
and the wall. Nothing to do but wait. Based on Stone's
letter, he wouldn't get a response until he came back
from his work on the lichgate tomorrow. For now, he
would sleep. Grateful or not, angry or not, he didn't
have the energy to deal with his not-father, anyway.

CHAPTER SIX

AGE 17

Late Summer
The Kingdom of Hillside

Cedric had hoped for a visit from Helen. He sat up in bed, eyes dropping as he struggled to stay awake, listening for the telltale rattle of the door handle.

She never came.

Instead, the door slammed open moments before the sun rose, waking him to the familiar scowl of the guard from yesterday. Yet again, he was nearly dragged through back allies. Yet again, the people of Hillside averted their eyes, ushered their children indoors, and left him alone. And yet again, he circled the lichgate for hours, humming to himself as if he were puzzling something complex. He asked to see the other lichgates, to which he received only a grunt in reply.

When the sun set, the guard once more shoved him into his bedroom. Once the door closed behind him, he sank onto the bed with a long sigh, rubbing his aching eyes. He longed to sleep and bathe and eat all at once, but the corner of another note stuck out from underneath his pillow.

He grabbed it and unfolded the parchment. Underneath the smudged lines of his charcoal message from yesterday, more of Stone's tight script covered the page.

Cedric—

   Yes, why don't I, an isen with only enough hyacinth to mask my scent for a week, change form and spend time around trained isen hunters? What could go wrong?

   Think before you suggest something, boy.

Cedric rolled his eyes, biting the inside of his cheek to stem his rising annoyance. He didn't have the patience or energy to deal with this man.

Still, he needed a plan, and Stone was his only hope. He continued reading.

Now, locking an entire kingdom's lichgates is certainly a challenge. How interesting. I've scouted the castle and for now, it's best to play along while I look for an opportunity to free you. Tell him you're making progress. He doesn't seem to be smart enough to realize you're doing nothing but walking around the lichgates while grumbling to yourself, so let's use his stupidity to our advantage. I'll solve this as we go. Locking the lichgates and offering keys to only a select few will limit accessibility dramatically and prevent anyone from entering unseen. I'll leave you instructions here as I come to understand how to accomplish this. It should keep that militant tart happy.

Try not to do anything stupid.

—Stone

Cedric shook his head. At least now they had a plan, but what actually annoyed him most was what Stone hadn't said. No acknowledgment of his gratitude or his warning. Just down to business, per usual.

With a groan, Cedric slumped on the bed. His head hit something hard beneath his pillow, and a jolt of pain shot down his neck. He cursed and reached for whatever had hurt him, only to find, much to his surprise, the milk-white gem Stone had used in his experiments on the lichgates back home.

Cedric studied the rock, a grateful smile spreading across his face despite his anger. The gem glowed faintly green in his palm, dimmed compared to its vibrant color when he'd held it back in Endervere.

A bit calmer, he reached for the pen.

Stone—

I'll wait for your instructions and will continue walking circles around the lichgates until then.

—Cedric

Maybe he should insist he had to see them all, study them all, before he get anywhere with it. That would buy him time while Stone came up with a real plan.

He returned the charcoal and note to his hiding place and sprawled on the mattress, staring at the ceiling. He should sleep, but he desperately wanted to go home. He wanted to return to his boring life, even if it meant continuing on as one of Stone's experiments. The anxiety of living under the roof of a man who wanted to kill him was starting to wear on his resolve.

In the hallway, floorboards creaked. Someone spoke in a hushed tone. Cedric sat upright, dread closing his throat as he wondered what they were discussing. He shoved the white rock in his pocket, tensing as the doorknob turned.

Helen entered, a broad smile on her face and two books in her hand.

Cedric beamed, part of him wondering if he was grinning like a fool. Too eager for her company. Too happy to see her. "I was worried you weren't going to find me again."

"I'm glad you enjoy my company, at least." She

laughed and sat on the edge of his bed, the mattress dipping slightly under her weight. She set the books beside her. He recognized one as the tome he'd hid under the mattress in his last cell: *A History of the Isen Plague*. Not the most charming read and quite inaccurate in some places, but the book offered an insightful look on how Hillsidians viewed isen culture and motivation. It would help Cedric frame his conversations with the Blood, if nothing else.

But the second surprised him. *A Theorized History of Ethos*. He'd never heard of Ethos before. He tapped the cover. "What's this?"

She chuckled. "Some light reading. It's an old myth about an ancient city where all six of the kingdoms lived together. It was a massive, mountain home called Ethos. There's no happy ending, since they disband and hate each other by the end, but the first half is lovely. It makes me wish that maybe someday our kingdoms can all live in peace, even if it's just a dream. I figured with the Blood's—er—overbearing personality, you might enjoy something lighthearted for a change, even if it's nothing but a bedtime story."

He smiled. "It sounds like a nice change of pace, actually."

She nodded, glancing about. "I'm glad Blood Tristan finally moved you to a proper room. That other one smelled terrible, but I didn't want to say anything. It wasn't like you had a choice."

Cedric shook his head. "It's what happens when you have a chamber pot in your bedroom."

She chuckled, and Cedric smiled. She caught his eye, that soft expression of hers returning. He wished he could place it, to understand what it meant, but at least he was able to enjoy it. To enjoy her.

The voice of reason spoke again in the back of his mind, warning him against trusting anyone. His smile fell. She seemed to know where he was, had access to his room despite the guards in the hallway—the mere fact that she came for him seemed too good to be true, too convenient to be real. After all, Blood Tristan owned everything and everyone in the castle. A beautiful face like Helen's could disarm a man. Hell, it had disarmed Cedric already. But she was perfect. Kind. Gentle. He didn't want to think she was anything less than genuine. With so few allies and no friends, he wanted to believe he could have at least one good connection in this deathtrap of a castle.

Still, thanks to the blood loyalty Blood Tristan wielded over his people, he could issue a command to any of his subjects to betray Cedric's deepest secrets. He had to be wary, even of Helen. He slumped at the realization, shoulders drooping with disappointment.

Her gaze fell to the floor. "Cedric..."

His heart leapt with panic, though he wasn't sure why. "What is it?"

She paused, lips parted for a few seconds as if she

were struggling to find words. "I have something to ask of you."

He waited, watching as her thick hair slid over her shoulders and a single strand fell across her eye. Whatever she was about to say, she seemed to dread it.

"Is it possible for you to remove my blood loyalty?" She lifted her dark eyes. They shook, as if terrified of what he would say.

Cedric frowned on impulse. A warning bell went off in his head, and he wondered again if she were nothing more than a spy trying to get him to say something incriminating, something that would get him killed.

She lifted her hands in gentle surrender. "I'm sorry. Maybe that was too forward. I—I'm sorry. Forget I said anything. I'm ..."

Her voice trailed off, and she stared again at the floor, tears brimming in her eyes. Cedric's frown dissolved, and with her tears, a bit of his resistance and reluctance went as well. A tear streaked down her cheek, and she wiped it away.

Cedric didn't know what to do. Stone had never taught him how to care for someone, or what to do when someone cried. Whenever Cedric hurt himself, Stone told him to walk it off, to get over it.

Pain is temporary, he would always say.

True, but it still left a scar. Cedric's childhood tears had always been met with indifference, but he wanted to be different than the man who'd raised him.

He set a hand on her shoulder, and Helen smiled briefly before wiping away the stream of water left on her cheek.

"Tell me why you would ask such a thing," Cedric said.

She sniffled and wrung her hands in her lap. "I'm about to be forced to do something I don't want to do."

Cedric could barely breathe. Dread shot through his veins like ice. "And that is?"

She sniffled. "It's a long story."

"It's not like I have anywhere to be."

She chuckled and caught his eye. He forced a smile, and she nodded. "I was genuinely curious to meet you, Cedric. I hope you know that. But yes, I came because I need something from you. I need to escape this place. The captain of the guard is a horrible man. He's killed so many, and not just isen. He has a lot of blood on his hands, and I'm not sure he's ever read a book. I never feel safe around him, even though he's supposed to protect us. I always feel like he's a beer away from hitting someone. Me, maybe. What's worse, he has recently started showing interest in me. He's told my father several times that he wants to bond with me, to make me his wife, and I stated just as many times that I'm not interested. I thought refusing him would be enough, but nothing goes unnoticed in his castle.

Rumors started recently, rumors about him and me. What scares me is Captain Alec is one of Blood Tristan's oldest friends. They grew up together, trained together. And if he asked Blood Tristan to … to …"

"You're worried he'll force you to bond with Captain Alec," Cedric finished for her.

She nodded furiously, wiping away more tears as she stared at the floor. "If my Blood commands me to, I will have no choice. I will have no control over my actions. That's why I envy you, Cedric. Even though you're a prisoner, you have a freedom none of us will ever know."

Cedric's heart shattered. He watched her gently sob on the edge of his bed, and his hand on her shoulder no longer seemed like enough. He pulled her close to him, wrapping his arms around her in a hug like he had seen so many husbands hold their wives during his visits to Endervere.

He held the back of her head and let her cry into his shoulder. "How much time do you have?"

"I don't know. My father convinced Captain Alec to at least give me space until I'm eighteen, saying I might change my mind as I get older. I won't, but it only gives me a few years. I've been trying to figure out what disgusts him, anything to make him realize that I won't make him happy, but he is as stubborn as he is stupid." She laughed.

Her slender hands wove around him, hugging him

in return, and everything in Cedric's core told him she was telling the truth. He wanted to say he knew how to help her. He wanted to write to Stone right then and ask how it could be done. But his life was at stake, and if he made a mistake with this girl, trusted her when he shouldn't, he would die. Blood Tristan wouldn't take kindly to Cedric trying to steal away his subjects. Cedric would be killed, probably in the most painful way possible to send a message to others hoping for the same freedom.

Seventeen years of Stone's voice in his head warned him again saying anything until he could be absolutely sure of her story.

"I don't know how to remove your blood loyalty," he said softly. It wasn't a lie, but it felt like one.

She watched him, her expression shifting from sadness to panic. Her lips parted, and she tried several times to say something, but only weak huffs of air escaped.

"I understand," she eventually said. She sniffled and stood, leaving the book on the bed.

"I'm sorry," he said, standing. He reached for her, part of him foolishly hoping another hug would help.

She smiled through her tears and set a hand on his arm. "It's okay. I thought with the timing of your arrival that maybe it was serendipity, but I was wrong. It's not your fault, and I'm a clever girl. Maybe I can come up with some other way to get out of this myself."

"I'll understand if you don't come back," he said, sticking his hands in his pockets.

She shook her head. "I enjoy your company, Cedric. I'll come back until it's too dangerous for me to do so. What book would you like next?"

He smiled, a cocktail of guilt, gratitude, affection, and respect swirling in his chest. "Surprise me."

She nodded and squeezed his hand gently before retreating from the room. He stared at the door long after her footsteps had faded from the hallway, wondering if he had done the right thing or doomed the only kind person he'd met in the capital to a life with a man she hated.

He sat on the bed, hands in his hair, and cursed quietly to himself. No wonder Stone didn't have any friends.

CHAPTER SEVEN

AGE 18

Late Summer
The Kingdom of Hillside

A year passed in what felt like days. The trees around the capital bled red, fell to the ground, and grew again in the spring. The forest around Hillside slept and awoke, and each day Cedric trudged through them to work on the Blood's lichgates, he came to love the capital a little bit more.

With the milk-white Stone had given him, Cedric examined each of the lichgates' energy. At first, the brilliant shades of purple it emitted meant nothing to him, but thanks to Stone, clues began to emerge as to what he needed to do next.

Stone's notes were helpful, to say the least. Written instructions, smudged occasionally because of the charcoal pen, guided Cedric through an otherwise impossible venture. Stone must have been running his own experiments, figuring out the process for himself mere days before he taught it to Cedric through his letters.

And each day, Cedric wondered when Stone would abandon him.

Each time Cedric came back to his room from a day out at the lichgates, he expected to find no note. In his heart, he always worried Stone would grow bored, frustrated, or simply leave again like he had so many times before. And yet, every night, there was a note with new instructions and—just as often—a fresh insult about something Cedric had done wrong the day before. Apparently, Stone was inspecting his work. Somehow.

No surprise there. Stone always possessed enough criticism to drown a sailor.

But each night also brought Helen. She brought food, books, and much needed company. The more they talked, the more he learned about her family and life in the capital. She'd never left, and he longed to show her Endervere.

He longed to break her blood loyalty.

Each passing night chipped away at his fears of betrayal and added to his guilt for not asking Stone how to do it. For the first time in his life, Cedric had a friend. And a gorgeous one, no less.

With time, she introduced him to her family—her eldest brother Emmett was a First Lieutenant in the Hillsidian castle guard, so the man had cashed in a few favors to switch guard duty. These last few months, Emmett had shared his war stories while Cedric took his breaks beneath the oak trees by the lichgates.

Cedric almost couldn't believe such luck could arise from a near death sentence. Thanks to his time as Blood Tristan's prisoner, he now had *two* friends.

On a particularly scalding, summer afternoon, Cedric knelt at the north-most lichgate, wiping the sweat from his brow as he paused for a moment and retreated to the shade of an oak tree. He leaned against it, the bark scratching his arm as he stared at the portal. Instead of a gate or a door, tangled metal vines stretched toward the sky and covered the lichgate. They would unravel only when someone passed through, and this posed the greatest challenge to him as he tried to lock the portal. He was used to gates and doors, yet these vines moved with a will of their own. When anyone neared, the vines would untangle them-selves in welcome, whistling and grating as the metal plants slid over each other to create an opening barely wide enough for him to walk through. For now, they remained closed as he debated a new development in the note he'd received last night from Stone.

Cedric tapped his cheek as he thought through how exactly to shift the energy enough to lock it without changing its end destination. He closed his eyes, recalling the instructions Stone had left for him, but he couldn't remember this part.

No doubt he would get a sarcastic note tonight about how long he was taking, but couldn't memorize it all. He groaned and slid to the ground, hand in his dirty hair as he yawned. He needed lunch and maybe a strong drink.

"Is the mighty Vagabond tired?" A man's voice came from the forest, and seconds later one of the guards emerged from the underbrush and sat beside Cedric. His dark skin contrasted the green and gold of his uniform, and the man's short, black hair framed his familiar square face. Cedric sighed with relief as he recognized Emmett. The soldier grinned, offering Cedric his canteen of water.

Cedric laughed, shaking his head as he took a sip. "The mighty Vagabond is frustrated."

"You're lucky I'm the only one on duty, then. I sent the rest off on fools' errands to buy you some time."

Cedric's shoulders drooped, and he ran his hand through his hair again, annoyed. He smacked the back of his head gently against the tree behind him, staring at the forest canopy as he tried to come up with a solution to his problem. "Locking the lichgates is taking forever."

"But you can do it, right?"

For a moment, Cedric debated the question. It

wasn't as if he had a choice. It was do or die, and he intended very much *not* to die. "I'll come up with something."

"You'd better."

With a quirked eyebrow and a grin, Cedric nudged his friend. "Oh, that's sweet, Emmett. I didn't know you cared."

Emmett stood, hooking his canteen on his belt. "Cute, kid. Cute. I'm more concerned for a certain young woman who enjoys your company and what would happen to her if you disappeared."

Cedric's smile fell, and he leaned his elbows on his knees as he stared at the dirt path wandering away from the lichgate. Helen. His heart skipped a beat at the mere thought of her, and he had to agree: at this point, he wanted to please the Blood as much for her sake as he did for himself.

Emmett crossed his arms, examining the canopy as he lowered his voice. "I haven't told her yet, but Captain Alec is back from the isen crusade."

Panicked, Cedric pushed himself to his feet. "He's back a full year earlier than expected. He can't possibly be done."

Emmett shook his head, rubbing his eyes as he began to pace the trail. "It seems like the isen guild he was hunting has changed their strategy. He claimed to be taking a break to recoup and strategize a counterattack. But almost as soon as he came back, he asked me about her."

Cedric tightened his hands into fists, frustrated with this man who would not give up when Helen made it so painfully clear for so long she was not interested in him. But he had childhood connections to the ruler, and the militant Blood Tristan often did favors for his friends. Rumors had begun circulating that Captain Alec had already asked for the Blood to command Helen to do what she didn't want to. "Why can't he get it through his thick skull—"

His friend shushed him. "Keep your voice low."

Cedric obeyed. "Fine, but why is he pressing this?"

Emmett frowned. "He's used to getting what he wants. Helen is my annoying little sister, but even I can admit she's one of the most beautiful women in Hillside. Captain Alec doesn't care about much else."

"How long does she have?"

"The law states no one can bond before they're eighteen. She has a year, less if Captain Alec gets impatient and asks for another favor."

Perfect. Fantastic. Cedric kicked the trunk of the nearest tree and cursed as pain shot up his foot. Frustrated, furious, he pulled on the ends of his hair. "What do I do? How do I stop this?"

Emmett set one hand on Cedric's shoulder, and Cedric was able to stand still long enough to catch the man's eye. "Finish the lichgate so that the Blood won't hunt you down as a fugitive, and then leave. Take her with you, and never come back."

Cedric's mouth parted, and he couldn't quite process what Emmett was asking him to do. "Leave? She grew up here. Her family is here. She loves you all."

A sad smile crossed Emmett's face, and he squeezed Cedric's shoulder. "Maybe so. But I know her, and if she stays here, she will lead a miserable life and die young. She's a bubble of joy and happiness, and she cannot thrive here anymore. She's attracted the wrong attention, and it's going to kill her if she's not careful. Her future isn't here, Cedric. It's with you. Promise me you'll do this. Promise me you'll take care of her, no matter what."

Cedric took a deep breath, holding Emmett's gaze as he processed exactly what the man was asking. He nodded, back arching. "I promise."

That night, Cedric sat on his bed with his back against the wall, his elbow resting on his knee as he watched Helen. She sat in a chair across from him, oblivious to his gaze as her eyes were buried in her own book. She had brought a novel tonight, instead of her usual history manual or research journal. Tonight's story was a mystery about two isen hunters who traveled Ourea. One of them had gone missing, and the other would find his partner at any cost. Helen gently bit the end of her nails, her body bent ever so slightly around the book as she lost herself to its story.

He adored this woman, and he couldn't imagine what he would do without her nightly visits. It had happened slowly, over hundreds of evenings, but she had captivated him completely. Shared with him. Trusted him. At some point, she had become crucial to his life working for the Blood, and he hadn't been able to put it into words until tonight.

Cedric loved her.

The elegant tilt of her neck sent a strand of her silky hair sliding toward her face, but she didn't seem to notice. Her eyes scanned the page of her book, and a small smile teased the corners of her lips.

"Why do you come here, Helen?"

It took a moment for Cedric to realize he'd spoken. It was such an odd question, one that hadn't registered in his mind before he spoke it. A pang of terror shot through him, and his heart raced as he feared her answer.

She lifted her gaze from the book, eyes locked on his, and quirked her eyebrow. "Beg your pardon?"

His impulse was to do as Stone so often did: ignore the question completely. Carry on as if he'd said nothing at all. He swallowed hard, seriously considering the option—after all, he wasn't sure he wanted to hear her answer. But if he waved away the thought like he wanted to, she would obsess over what he'd meant and likely walk away with the wrong impression. He couldn't bear for her to think he didn't want her here.

No way out now. He had to clarify. "You come here every night, bring me books and food and company. I've never met anyone so simultaneously brilliant and beautiful, and yet you're here. With me. I can't imagine why."

Her pursed lips bled into a smile, and relief washed through Cedric, if only for a moment. She still hadn't answered. He could be a mildly interesting way to pass her time, or an experiment, or—

His heart skipped a beat, and he studied his hands for a moment. After a lifetime with Stone for a father, he didn't need to be anyone else's experiment.

"You've never courted a woman, have you?" Helen sat back in her chair, ankles crossed and tucked around one of the chair legs. She grinned, her eyes lit with mischief.

Cedric's mouth went dry, and he wondered what the hell kind of game she was playing. "You didn't answer my question."

"I will. Answer mine."

"So, commanding," he said with a chuckle.

She lifted her chin, impish smile still in place, and waited.

He let loose a playful sigh. "No, I haven't."

"No girls in your village who caught your eye?"

Cedric ran his tongue along his back molars, trying to find words that wouldn't make her think less of him. None came. He opted for the truth. "I didn't catch their eyes. They preferred the hunters. The soldiers."

Helen's smile fell, and he was certain his honesty had made her realize her mistake. How foolish to hope she was different, or that—

She stood, and panic flooded his chest. This was it. She would leave, now. He struggled to breathe, but he reined in his terror at the thought of losing the one woman whose company he'd enjoyed. Whatever happened, whatever came next, he could handle it.

But Helen surprised him. Instead of heading for the door, she sat on the bed beside him. The mattress dented beneath her, and she scooted a bit closer as she settled in. She was so close—too close. Her smooth hair was within reach, begging for him to tuck it behind her ear. He craved her.

She nudged him. "I prefer the scholars. The leaders. Cedric, I prefer you."

He swore his heart stopped. This couldn't be real. Smart, charming, gorgeous women from the capital didn't want him. He was dreaming, or worse, dead.

"Why would you want a broken traitor?" he blurted out.

Her lips parted, and a blur of emotions crossed her face—sadness, affection, maybe a hint of pity. He couldn't follow them all. "Cedric, you're not broken."

She paused, and a giggle escaped her. "But I am quite enamored by the fact that you're a traitor."

He laughed along with her, admiring the rich color of her skin and the dazzling eyes that drew him in, daring him to do what he'd wanted to do since he first saw her. He reached a hand for her cheek, and when she didn't stop him, he kissed her.

Her fingers wove through his hair, and her sweet breath rushed along his face. Joy, pride, victory—they burned in his core, growing stronger every second the kiss lasted. His hands found her waist, and he pulled her closer, tugging her across the bed toward him. She laughed and pulled away, her nose still touching his as he looked into her warm eyes. He ran a hand through her hair, careful not to speak lest he ruin this.

"Don't you dare think you're broken, Cedric," she said softly. Her angelic voice drew him in, and he set his forehead on hers, eager to be close, to touch her, to know this was real.

"I have no blood loyalty, Helen. I'm an anomaly. I'm... I'm a ..."

"You have a gift, and if you waste it, you'll fail yourself and the people you were put on this world to help."

He set his hands on her shoulders and leaned back until her face came fully into focus once more. "What do you mean?"

"You call yourself broken, but you have the one thing every Hillsidian in this city has prayed for at some point in his or her life. You see an 'anomaly,' but I see a leader. A talented man who's going to change the world if he only believes he's capable."

Cedric didn't know what to say. No one had ever talked to him like this, believed in him this much. The panic in his chest smoldered until it became an intense sense of calm, accompanied by a warmth that reminded him of embers in a dying fireplace. It was a moment of knowing, of understanding, as if something in his body had shoved aside all the fear for a moment and said, *yes, finally.*

He was broken, yes, but perhaps for a reason. Perhaps he could do some good in this world, help those who longed for what he had.

This was his truth.

His purpose.

Helen's eyes shifted back and forth between his. "I can't read your expression, Cedric. What's going through your—"

He pulled her into a rough kiss, his lips pressing against hers as he ached to thank her, to pour this new sense of certainty into her, to show her what it meant to him to have someone believe in him. He wanted to protect her, cherish her, do anything at all to show his gratitude.

She paused, lips grazing his jaw as she bumped his cheek with her nose. "So, what'll it be?"

He fought for the words to express this flux of

emotion. "I don't know why I am the way I am, what happened to me or if it can be undone, but you're right. It's mine, and Blood Tristan feared me enough to want to kill me. Maybe the others will fear me, too—which means I have power. I can give people hope. I can change the way things are."

"We'll do it together," she said.

He grinned so widely it hurt his face. "Nothing would make me happier."

CHAPTER EIGHT

AGE 18

Late Autumn
The Kingdom of Hillside

I t took three more months of incessant prodding in a bit of back-and-forth cursing between him and Stone, but they did it. With Stone's help and Emmett's encouragement, Cedric had locked the northern lichgate.

In the autumn air and with Emmett beside him, Cedric stepped back to examine the lichgate from the outside, standing on the dirt trail that led up to what was once the most obvious lichgate into the city—a sunny portal between two trees in a dark forest. Now, however, he faced nothing but an eternal forest filled with thick oak trees. Fog rolled through the under-brush, thick as smoke. A chill swept through him, but he grinned with victory. There was no indication of a lichgate whatsoever.

"Let's hope we can get back," Emmett said under his breath.

"Oh, ye of little faith," Cedric said.

As the final test, he pulled an ornate brass key from his pocket, one the Blood had given him through a grapevine of soldiers and orders. Cedric hadn't spoken to the man in months, and he preferred it that way. The key's cold metal reminded him of the doorknob of his childhood home, and he rubbed it with his thumb for good luck. He'd charmed it to work on this lichgate and this lichgate only, and it was time to see if he and Stone were as clever as they thought.

Cedric pressed a gnarled old knot in one of the nearest trees, and the spring embedded in its bark snapped to life. The knot opened on hinges to reveal a hidden keyhole in the wood. Cedric set the brass key into the hole and twisted, eyes ahead as he waited, breathless, for success.

A broad ray of green light cascaded across them. The edges of the forest blurred. A new, greener avenue of pine trees and a cobblestone road appeared before them where decaying trunks had been before. Golden vines towered above him, tangled in an intricate metal wall that hid the lichgate at the end of the path, its thick, golden rods carved to look like vines of ivy. The vines untangled themselves in welcome as he neared, whistling and grating as the metal plants slid over each other. They unwound to create an opening barely wide enough for the two of them to pass.

Emmett hollered and pumped his fist in the air. "Scholars are good for something!"

Cedric laughed, hands on his hips as he admired his handiwork. Amazing. Over year ago, he'd pulled this idea from thin air, desperate to keep himself alive and with no idea if it would work. And now, he had succeeded. He and Stone had done the impossible.

They had locked a lichgate. A royal one at that.

"I'll tell the Blood," Emmett said. "In the meantime, I'll take you back to your room. He'll want to talk to you, but you may have to wait a bit. Excellent job, my friend."

Cedric grinned, as happy with Emmett's complement as he was with what he had accomplished.

Back in his room, Cedric leaned against the wall and stared out his window, heart racing as he wondered what the Blood would say. Blood Tristan hadn't looked up from the papers on his desk last time they spoke, apparently absorbed in whatever notes or maps he'd been reviewing. For others, the king's growing disinterest would have spelled disaster. For Cedric, it was marvelous news. It meant Blood Tristan would soon think of him as a trivial matter, something not worth his time, and let him go.

Hopefully.

The door swung open and hit the wall with a thud. Cedric spun around in time to catch an old man slam the door shut behind him. He held towels and a simple, metal tray with a few strips of meat and a loaf of bread balanced on top of it.

"Oh, thank you," Cedric said. He reached for the tray to help the old man and set it on the bed.

The servant frowned, brows furrowed with a hint of annoyance that reminded Cedric of Stone. He opened his mouth to speak, but the edges of the man's body began to shimmer in a familiar way. Cedric flinched, caught off guard. Only isen could ...

... oh.

The wrinkles on the old man's face melted away like wax off a candle, and dark hair sprouted through his otherwise bald head. He grew taller, his back straighter, and in seconds Stone stood where the old man had been.

Cedric lowered his voice to a harsh whisper, eyes on the door even as frustration burned within him. "What are you doing? You can't be here. The guards will be back any minute. And what did you—you stole some old man's soul? What's wrong with you?"

Stone grunted in disgust. "You are so very welcome

for all of my help over this past year. Do try to show a bit of gratitude."

Hands lifted in slight surrender, Cedric backed away. The old man's soul was gone, and it wasn't as though Stone could release it. Not until his death. He had done what he'd had to do, and Cedric could only appreciate the effort. "Fine. Fair argument. Thank you, Stone. You have done so much for me, and I'm grateful."

"Much better. And I will say, locking that lichgate is my finest work."

Cedric paused, eyes on the floor. "Better than me?"

When no answer came, Cedric summoned the courage to catch his mentor's eye, only to find the isen watching him again in the same manner he regarded his experiments—cautiously, detached from the outcome, and as if waiting for him to explode.

But no matter how much he wanted to scream, to demand an answer, Cedric would not lose control. Not here, not when the guards could come in at any moment and interrupt them.

"It's time to leave," Stone said.

A blast of surprise shot through Cedric, shattering his annoyance and frustration. "What do you mean? We've only locked one of the lichgates."

"They have the concept now. They can do it them-selves. It's impressive, but not impossible to replicate."

"W-what about me, then? Can you replicate me?"

Stone paused, and Cedric saw for the first time an expression of confusion run across the old isen's face. He'd seen plenty of curiosity and disgust over the years, but never confusion. It set Cedric's nerves ablaze with anxiety.

This was the question he had avoided all his life. Stone owed him an answer, even if he didn't want to know what it was, where he'd come from, or what Stone had done to him as a child.

"We don't have time for this," Stone said.

"Answer my question."

"Well, what the devil are you asking?"

Cedric huffed with annoyance. "How do I turn other yakona into vagabonds like me?"

"Ah," Stone said, rubbing his beard. "They do call you that here, don't they? Such a strange title. You want to remove the blood loyalty from others, as you believe I removed yours."

"Didn't you?" Cedric's throat ran dry, but he arched his back and refused to look away from the not-father who'd raised him.

Stone let out a long, slow sigh and rubbed his eyes. He opened his mouth several times, but nothing ever came out. His jaw tensed, and it seemed for all the world like he wanted to say something but didn't know how.

"Can you do it or not?" Cedric's voice came out softer than he intended, quieter and calmer than he felt. It might have been anxiety, or the fear of the answer, or his gratitude for everything else Stone had done, good or bad, that made Cedric the person he was today. He didn't want to be cruel or unfair to the not-father whom he respected despite his better judgment. Cedric simply wanted the truth.

Stone nodded.

Cedric's heart leapt with joy. "Teach me."

The isen rolled his eyes. "Fine, yes, in my experiments, I stumbled across the discovery. But it's a dangerous one, Cedric. Isen and yakona alike have died."

A chill raced down Cedric's spine. "You've killed people?"

Stone groaned. "I'm not proud of it. They were casualties of academia. Why do you think I leave to run my experiments? I knew you couldn't handle the truth. You would've gotten in the way. But progress is made through blood, sweat, and sacrifice. Of course, some have died to teach me what I know."

Cedric could barely fathom their conversation. This couldn't be happening. "What the hell kind of research have you been doing?"

"We're getting off topic—"

"Stone, answer me! Why would—"

"You know I have my own master, and you know how long I've been running from him," Stone said quietly.

Cedric hesitated, unable to breathe as the words sunk in. Stone never spoke much about his life before the house on the outskirts of Endervere, but what he did share involved a lot of isen and even more death. Stone had the misfortune of belonging to a guild of cutthroats all run by single man, but his not-father never spoke the master's name. Stone had escaped that life not so long ago, and he feared being forced to return.

It was the one thing Stone deeply feared.

A realization crashed over Cedric, setting the nerves in his fingers ablaze with fury. "So, you been running experiments on other isen, trying to break their connection to their master in an effort to break your own. And you've failed. That's why the book has so much blood—"

Stone cut him off. "Yes, yes, I know. You disapprove. And so far, I've learned too little about isen and too much about yakona. But I'm determined. He can't control me forever."

Cedric ran a hand through his hair, pacing as he tried to sift through all this new information. His mind wandered to Helen, to Emmett, to his cause. As much as he loathed his not-father for killing people—likely innocents, at least for the yakona—he needed to focus. He couldn't change the past, couldn't bring back those Stone had killed. Instead, he needed to keep his attention on his future. To those he could still help.

With a sigh, Cedric pinched the bridge of his nose to stem his anger. "Fine. Teach me how to break a yakona's blood loyalty."

"I don't see the benefit," Stone said.

"Not everything has to have a benefit for you!"

Stone shrugged. "Doesn't it? Besides, what possible benefit is there for you? What's the benefit for these people you turn? *Bloods*, Cedric, why do you even care?"

"I—well ..."

"Spit it out, boy."

Cedric lifted his chin in defiance. "These people are slaves, and you always told me that was wrong. You always told me controlling someone's will was the worst injustice we could do to anyone, and yet, this slavery is built into who these people are. Their Blood can force them to obey, can change their opinions. Those boys Blood Tristan took from our village for the isen wars? Half of them have disappeared, probably because their souls were stolen by the isen they were hunting."

"Serves them right," Stone said, shrugging.

Cedric rubbed the back of his neck, doing everything he could not to scream at his not-father. "The point is they didn't have a choice, Stone. They were forced into the life of an isen hunter, and this is no way to live. I just want to bring peace to this world, to these people."

Stone groaned, eyes flitting to the door before he spoke. "You can't turn every yakona in the world. There are too many, and you're only one man. This seems like a silly dream more than something you can actually accomplish. Do you have a plan? Any allies? Any solid reason at all to even do this?"

"My plan," Cedric said, emphasizing the word, "is to get the Blood to be peaceable, to respect the responsibility in his authority rather than abuse it. I'm the only yakona in this world who doesn't have a blood loyalty. No matter what you did to me to make me this way, I can help people. They need me."

"I bet that's a nice feeling," Stone said dryly.

"What do you mean—"

"Enough, enough." Stone waved away Cedric's question. "If you want Blood Tristan to be peaceful, why bother changing anyone?"

"I can't do this alone, but I can't trust anyone with a blood loyalty. Their Blood could turn them on me at any moment."

The old isen quirked an eyebrow, tilting his head slightly. "Good point. Still, it's stupid to rely on people. They will only disappoint you."

"Not these people. Helping them means everything to me, Stone. Please, will you teach me what I need to know to protect them?"

Stone closed his eyes, shaking his head slightly as he rested his hands on his hips. "With what are you asking of me, I can never understand why you call me selfish."

"Stone!"

"Very well, I will help you on occasion."

Despite his stewing anger and disgust at Stone's methods, Cedric smiled with relief. "Thank you. Thank you!"

The isen nodded. "It seems as though you're going to do it anyway, so I may as well keep you from getting yourself killed. Keep in mind I have my own experiments to do, so I won't be available at your beck and call. Especially if this goes on for very long."

"This isn't an experiment. It's a movement," Cedric said, his smile faltering.

"Everything is an experiment until it succeeds."

"Stone—"

"Well, let's get a move on. We don't need to stay here a moment longer. I would like to get out of the city of isen hunters, personally."

"I can't leave yet." Cedric crossed his arms to drive home his point. He couldn't leave without Helen, and all of his contacts were in the city.

"Oh, for Bloods' sake, boy. You're impossible," Stone muttered.

Footsteps echoed down the hallway.

In a blast of panic, Cedric ushered Stone toward the bathroom door. If a guard entered, Stone could at least hide until the threat passed. The isen skidded along the floor, grumbling as he resisted. Cedric flexed his muscles, tightening his core as he pushed harder, and Stone slid closer to the bathroom.

"Will you stop?" the isen hissed.

"I'm trying to save you—"

Stone shook his head and lowered his voice. "Don't be ridiculous. Look, Cedric. I enjoyed this experiment, but it's done and I'm ready for the next. How long are you going to pretend you're a prisoner here? You will always be a threat, no matter what you do for this Blood. Take your place as a real danger and stop placating a murderous king who's trying to cling to his power. He will kill you, Cedric, the moment you're no longer useful."

Cedric swallowed hard, trying desperately to ignore the anxiety twisting in his gut at the mere thought of Blood Tristan. In his heart, he knew he would never be released. But it didn't make what he had to do any less important. "I understand, but I need you to show me how to change yakona before you leave. Stay for one more night. Please."

The isen sighed. "Very well, since you seem determined to do stupid things, I'll indulge you. That bulky guard friend of yours is on duty tonight. Will he have a problem with any of this?"

Arms crossed to hide his excitement, Cedric shook his head.

"I'll be here around midnight. Whomever you want

to change, make sure he's here by then. This procedure will hurt him immensely, but it seems like the end result will be worth the pain. See to it you choose this person wisely, Cedric."

Stone shifted again into the old man, his form shrinking as he hobbled toward the door. It clicked shut behind him as he left, and Cedric breathed in a long sigh of relief. A part of him was disgusted by the fact Stone had done something so apparently painful to him as a child, but Cedric had gotten what he wanted: the truth and a way out. There was only one yakona he had in mind to be the first person he changed, and he had no doubt in his mind what her answer would be when he asked.

CHAPTER NINE

AGE 18

Late Autumn
The Kingdom of Hillside

Several hours after the sunset, Cedric paced room with his hands behind his back. Any moment now, Helen would enter his room with a new book and a small feast like she always did. But as he wandered the tiny space in his room, the same thoughts ran over and over through his mind: *what would she say? Would they get caught? What if someone replaced Emmett tonight?*

A light tap came at his door, and it creaked open a second later. Helen entered, smiling broadly, a pack over her shoulder with a long thin loaf of bread sticking out of the top. Without pausing, she dropped her bag on the floor and wrapped her arms around his neck, pulling him into a deep kiss. Her fingers ran through his hair, and his anxiety melted away at her touch. For several seconds, he forgot all his worry, all his concern, and he simply lost himself in the warmth of her body pressed against his.

"Congratulations on locking the lichgate," she said, smiling.

Oh, of course. With the excitement of his conversation with Stone, Cedric had at all but forgotten his achievement of the day. The Blood hadn't even called him to his office to discuss it and learning how to break someone's blood loyalty seemed so much more important.

He cleared his throat and set his hands on Helen's shoulders. "I have something very important to tell you."

"What is it?" Her eyes widened, her lips parting ever so slightly. He was tempted to kiss her again, drawn in by his smooth lines of her face, but he resisted the impulse.

His throat ran dry, but he forced the words out. "I can break your blood loyalty."

Her smile fell. She didn't say anything.

"If you still want me to," he added.

"But you said …" Her voice was barely a whisper, cracking as she spoke.

"I know. I know."

"Did you lie to me?" Her brows twisted, and she stepped back, hands on her chest as her eyes locked with his.

His gut churned with familiar guilt, but he shook his head. "I don't personally know how, not yet. My mentor does, and he's going to teach me tonight. He's going to teach me by turning you."

She stood a little straighter, her thin wrists rising ever so slightly, blocking his view of her neck as they rested under her chin, elbows tucked close to her body. He'd seen her do this before, usually when she was sad or early on in their friendship when she was too afraid to ask for the comfort of a hug. It was her way of closing off, protecting herself.

Cedric gently set his fingers on her elbows, pulling her toward him as tenderly as he could manage. "I'm not going to force you to do anything you don't want to do. This is your choice, and I trust you. I trust you not to tell anyone even if you don't go through with it."

Her eyes drifted to the floor, and for a moment she didn't move. She didn't even breathe. She stared at the floorboards, a nail grazing her lip as Cedric waited for an answer.

When she finally spoke, it was in the barest whisper. "Will it hurt?"

"I'm afraid so," Cedric said.

"Will you be with me?"

He pulled her in close, wrapping her in a hug she didn't reciprocate. "I'll never leave your side."

Slowly, her hands wove around his back and returned the embrace. Her nails dug into his shirt, but he didn't mind the pressure. He was simply grateful she didn't seem angry anymore.

The door creaked open, and Helen gasped. Cedric spun her away from the door, putting himself between her and whomever was entering, but a familiar old man hobbled in with a tattered book in his hands and a pack over his shoulder. He studied Helen for a moment, brow quirking in apparent surprise. Cedric glared at him, daring him to say anything, but the still-disguised Stone simply shook his head.

"Let's get this over with," he said, voice warbling with age.

Cedric's grip around Helen tightened on impulse, but this was it. The moment of truth. He had trusted her with one of his greatest secrets, something that could get him killed if it was discovered, and now she had to choose.

"So, what will it be?" he asked her.

She held him while staring at the old man as he set a bottle and a rag at the foot of the bed next to his frayed book. Her fingers curled against his back, scooping up a handful of his shirt as she no doubt debated her options.

"Helen," he prodded.

"I'm sorry. I know I asked for this, but now that it's here, now that it's possible, I don't know what to do. I thought it would never happen and wrote it off as an option. I wasn't expecting this, so I'm just scared. I don't know what the consequences are."

"It's okay. It's a big decision."

"One I had assumed was already made," the still-disguised Stone said curtly, arms crossed as he stood at the foot of the bed.

"Your mentor is older than I expected," she whispered.

"Oh, he's not—"

Stone cleared his throat loudly, and it suddenly clicked for Cedric as to why Stone hadn't shifted form yet. To Stone, Helen was a stranger no matter how much Cedric trusted her. Stone didn't want her to know he was an isen, and since he was doing Cedric such a favor, Cedric supposed he could hold onto this one truth for now and share it with her later.

"Let's do this," she said, lifting her chin to catch his eye.

He smiled. "Are you sure?"

She nodded. "I trust you. We're in this together, right?"

"Right," he said softly, tucking a lock of her hair behind her ear.

Stone grumbled something Cedric didn't catch. The

isen rolled his eyes and grimaced, the wrinkles on his face deepening.

It didn't matter. Cedric was grateful to have someone as supportive as Helen on his side. He led her to the bed, and she sat. Her hands trembled in her lap, and he set his palms over top of them, willing her to be calm. He smiled again, as genuinely and reassuringly as he could, and she returned it.

"Hold out your hand," the disguised Stone said.

She obliged. Quick as lightning, Stone pricked her pointer finger. A pool of her green blood appeared on her delicate skin.

"Stone!" Cedric grabbed Helen's hand and pulled her toward him, shielding her from whatever the hell his not-father had done to her.

"Relax," Stone said with a frustrated grumble.

"Ow," Helen said, sucking on her finger.

"You just—"

Stone waved away Cedric's complaint. "You must test the blood before and after. She has a Hillsidian blood loyalty, and thus her blood is green. If this works, her blood will become red, like yours."

Helen shifted her gaze to Cedric, eyes widening in surprise. "You bleed red?"

Cedric's jaw tensed, but he nodded.

Stone opened his book and flipped through several blood-stained pages. "We can't waste time. Is this happening or not?"

Cedric hesitated, eyes on the bloody book, but it was now or never. He held her face, resisting the urge to kiss her. "Ready?"

"Ready," she said with a smile.

CHAPTER TEN

AGE 18

Late Autumn
The Kingdom of Hillside

Thirty minutes later, Cedric stood at the foot of his bed, watching Helen as she slept thanks to the sleeping aid Stone had brought along in the bottle. Her chest fell and rose in a steady rhythm. A bead of red blood pooled on her fingertip, and Cedric wiped it away.

Stone paced the room in his natural form. He'd changed as soon as he'd held the tonic-drenched rag to Helen's mouth and nose. He now hummed to himself as he reviewed his notes, scratching his cheek and muttering to himself. Before long, he slammed the book shut. "That's everything. You remember it all?"

Cedric nodded. "All yakona operate on a similar

energy level to their Blood, which allows for their connection with him. It's the same concept as the lichgates—two lichgates are connected across the world when they operate at the same energy level. So, what I have to do is change the energy level to operate at one above its current level. She'll still hear the Blood, but she won't have to obey."

"Good. And the process itself?"

"I fuse the white gem with the base of the neck, right along the spine. By twisting the gem clockwise until the color changes, I can raise the energy level. The process breaks the blood loyalty connection, but I can only change it by a single shade or I'll kill the person I'm trying to help. Test the blood before and after."

"Correct. And afterward?"

Cedric grimaced. He hated this part. "Let them sleep until the tonic wears off, or else they'll wake up screaming."

"That's everything. I think you've got it."

Nerves twisted in Cedric's gut. He hated to have lives resting so literally in his hands. So much relied on him adjusting everything with exact care. "Can I—uh—can I have that book?"

Stone groaned, but he eventually offered the ratty old tome. Cedric reached for it, smiling with gratitude.

The isen withdrew the book at the last moment, frowning. "You were nervous when I was by her neck."

Cedric hesitated. "I don't know what you mean."

"Don't play stupid, boy. It's not your strong suit. You're worried I was going to steal her soul."

Cedric scratched his head in an effort to look away and distract himself from Stone's intense gaze, but the old man was right. It had taken every ounce of self-control not to shove Stone away from her the moment he'd set a hand on her neck. Cedric had seen Stone steal a soul twice in his short life thus far, and it was a terrifying affair. The fear of losing someone as precious to him as Helen, even to someone as important as his not-father, had made him almost irrational.

Stone shoved the bottle and rag into the pack he had brought with him. "Foolish boy. I'm quite picky about the souls I steal. She didn't make the cut, and I doubt she ever will. You have nothing to worry about from me."

Cedric's eye twitched with annoyance at his mentor's trivialization, but he didn't press the issue.

Backpack slung over his shoulder, Stone paused in front of Cedric and once more offered the book. This time, the isen watched him with narrowed eyes and a slight grimace—an emotion different from his familiar usual disgust or annoyance. For a moment, Cedric wondered if this could be concern.

Without a word, he set the white gem in Cedric's hand. It glowed faintly green at his touch.

"Thank you, Stone."

The isen nodded. "Try not to die."

Cedric frowned. Stone walked around him, headed for the door. Cedric spun, his mouth moving faster than his brain. "Wait."

Stone paused. "Yes?"

"Why did you do this to me? You did this to me when I was a baby, didn't you?" He pointed to Helen's sleeping form.

The isen shook his head. Yet again, he seemed to struggle with words, taking too long to articulate thoughts he had certainly already pieced together by now. Cedric waited, but Stone eventually sighed. "I will tell you one day. Ask me in ten years and see if my answer still matters."

"What—why won't you simply tell me? Is it so horrible?"

Stones eyebrows twisted, and an expression of deep disappointment crossed his face. "Not horrible. Merely distracting. In the meantime, I do have a gift for you. Something I've been working on for a few years now."

Stone set his hands on Cedric's temples. Cedric tried to lift his hands, to bat the isen away and ask for more info, but a sharp pain blistered through his skin where his not-father touched him. The agony rooted him in place. He tried to yell, to wriggle away, but he could only arch his back and grit his teeth. He squeezed his eyes shut, lungs near bursting as he struggled to breathe.

What the hell is he doing to me?

The blood in Cedric's veins seemed to boil, scorching from within. Pins and needles ravaged every inch of his body. Sweat dripped down his back in little rivers. Rational thought faded. He wanted to claw at the hands on his face, beg for Stone to stop. He'd spoken out of turn, angered Stone, and this was his punishment. It had to be.

Unable to take it any longer, he opened his mouth to scream. Guards be damned. He needed this to end, and he would yell until someone came to stop it.

But he couldn't. His lungs wouldn't obey. Instead, he stretched open his mouth in a silent screech. It was all he could manage.

All at once, everything settled. The hands lifted from his temples, and Cedric slumped to the floor. Chest heaving, nausea burned his throat. A bead of sweat dropped into his eye. He rubbed his face, sucking in breath after breath as he tried to regain his composure.

Cedric let out a string of curses, not caring who heard.

"Hush, boy. The guards will hear you."

It was all Cedric could do not to punch Stone in the nose. "*Bloods!* W-what did you do to me?"

"I gave you a gift."

"You about killed me, you mean. Bloods, do you realize how painful that was?"

Stone crossed his arms. "I apologize. I didn't realize what a delicate flower you are."

Cedric tried to stand, desperate to shake some sense into his not-father or maybe hurl something at the man's head, but the room spun. Cedric stumbled, setting one hand on the wall as another bought of nausea shot up his throat. He swallowed, doing his best to calm himself in an effort to swallow the pain. "Tell me what you did to me. Right now."

"I gave you a new ability, one I discovered on accident in my research. It allows you to see someone's most influential memory, the moment that makes a man who he is now. To access it, you need to focus. I learned it while studying other isen, and it relates directly to our ability to access the soul. But instead of stealing it, you're simply opening the mind to see a single memory. It should be enough to keep you from trusting the wrong people."

"And you didn't think a warning was necessary? Or perhaps asking if I even wanted it?"

"Why bother? You need to be equipped with the techniques and tools to succeed. You're welcome. Honestly, sometimes I can't even understand what gets you so upset."

Cedric shook his head and set his hands on the wall, back to Stone to refrain from hurling something at the man's head. To distract himself, Cedric stared at his arms. Aside from the queasiness, he didn't feel any different than before the pain, but Stone had obviously done something to him. "How many isen did you kill to learn this memory technique?"

"You ask the wrong questions, Cedric."

"But—"

"This is easier for isen to pick up, since it's natural to us, but I know you'll learn it quickly. You simply have to focus, ask the person's mind for what it is you want to know. Go on, try it on her." Stone nodded to Helen, asleep in Cedric's bed.

"No! This is such a violation of trust, and you didn't even ask me if—*Bloods*, Stone, and while she sleeping, without even asking—"

"For God's sake, boy, you are such a frustrating child. Here." He thrust his arm forward and stared out the window, scowling.

Cedric tensed, his hand hovering over Stone's exposed forearm. He set his finger on his not-father's skin and waited.

Nothing happened.

Stone huffed with annoyance. "Don't be lazy about it. Focus. Ask my mind for the memory, and it will have no choice but to obey."

Cedric gritted his teeth, sweeping aside his fears and thoughts of Helen's hair splayed across his pillow. He closed his eyes and reached for the outcome—a memory—with his mind as he so often did with his magic, trying to connect with Stone's thoughts in a way that would yield a result.

Any result. *Something.*

The light in the room drained with a sudden rush, like water down a drain. Gold and white wisps sprang from the floor and circled around him, streaking across the now black room in thick strokes as they painted pale outlines of buildings in a town Cedric didn't recognize.

Other wisps carved out rumbling carts and a street, each of the white lines whizzing through the darkness and leaving a hazy imprint in its wake. As the road formed, he walked through a crowd, no longer in control of his own body. A man glanced over as Cedric joined the throng, but his attention lasted barely a second. In moments, Cedric was no longer worth examining. Nothing more than another peasant in the throng.

He smiled. The thrill of hope lit his chest. Freedom. A blast of hatred followed for a man whose name Cedric had never heard—Niccoli. Without understanding how, he knew Niccoli was his—Stone's—master. A man without mercy. And though he wasn't free of Niccoli yet, he was close. So close. He would be safest out of the city, and if he correctly recalled how they had entered, he needed to head north. Beyond that, he didn't care where he went as long as it was away from the isen he hated most.

Bodies surrounded him, and he took a deep breath to center himself in the masses. Sweat and urine wafted from the crowd like spoiled cologne. He wanted nothing more than to escape the throng and its stink, but he had to blend in. He kept his head down to avoid being seen. Men walked past, some accompanied by women, and the occasional cart split the crowd.

Another man walked up beside him and kept pace. Stone turned his head away, enough to hide most of his face, but the stranger didn't move past him. He matched Stone's gait.

"Are you enjoying your stroll?" Niccoli asked, his voice echoing in the memory. His thick accent marred his words, slurring them together. *Yor strohll.*

Cedric let out a long breath and stopped midstride. The crowd parted. One man smacked his shoulder. Several voices speaking a language he didn't understand complained as he stood in the middle of the road, redirecting a flood of people around him.

The crowds flowed past, frowning and shaking fists in his periphery. He didn't care. Niccoli pulled ahead and stopped, his familiar, dark hair and pale skin like an anchor tearing through Cedric's hope. The isen master waited, hands in his pockets as he smirked.

Sweat pooled along Cedric's hairline. "How do you always know where I am?"

"I own you, boy," Niccoli said with a shrug.

Light returned around Cedric in a sudden, intense

flash as he pulled free from Stone's memory. Cedric blinked, spots on his vision as he tried to process what he'd seen. The warm tone of the wood walls and floor centered him, anchoring him back in the present. He didn't know what to say. Stone had always been so no-nonsense, so certain and absolute. To get a glimpse into what he was so long ago, to see the moment that had changed him so completely, convinced him to run away and do everything in his power to stop his connection to Niccoli—Cedric suddenly felt as though he understood his not-father in an entirely new way.

"Thank you," Cedric said, eyes on the wall to avoid looking at his mentor.

Stone grunted. "Hopefully this will protect you and help you see the intentions and motivations of the people around you. Because for someone so smart, you can be an absolute idiot. You're too damn trusting. You need to leave this place as soon as possible. Don't linger, don't wait. Leave."

Without another word, Stone shifted once more into the old man. Skin fell away like wax off a candle, and he shrank. He threw the bag once more over his back and left, the door slamming behind him.

Cedric watched the door long after Stone had disappeared. Part of him wanted to celebrate, and the other part wanted to vomit out of sheer anxiety. He had learned how to break a yakona's blood loyalty. Helen would never have to bond with Captain Alec, and Cedric could finally start the movement that would change Ourea forever.

He knelt beside her, resting his chin on the mattress by her face. If Stone was right, the Blood planned to kill Cedric sooner rather than later—and more disappointing was the fact that Stone was rarely wrong. He had planned to impress the Blood, to change the man's mind, but it seemed that was no longer possible.

The plan had changed. He and Helen had started a revolution, even if only the two of them knew about it, and he had a duty to see it through to the end.

In her sleep, she whimpered. He ran his thumb along her cheek, and she stilled. This was no small task they had taken on, and they were about to go head-to-head with the most powerful people in all of Ourea. He knew it was the right thing to do, but it didn't make it any less terrifying.

He hoped against hope that at the end of this tunnel was a happy ending for them both.

CHAPTER ELEVEN

AGE 19

Late Autumn
The Kingdom of Hillside

A year passed.

Cedric waited, sitting on the edge of his bed, staring at the door as the minutes ticked by. He lingered on the edge of the bed, awaiting the signal that it was safe to leave—that the guards had switched, and his allies were ready to sneak him out.

The year had gone by too quickly. He had stalled in his locking of the other lichgates, making up reasons why he couldn't finish them quicker now that he had done one successfully. By using large words Blood Tristan didn't understand—mostly those Cedric had made up himself—he was often dismissed with nothing more than the command to hurry it up already. But the king was growing impatient. Rumors swarmed the castle, suffocating Cedric with nerves as the chattering servants all agreed—the Blood had little patience left for the Vagabond.

With each delay, Cedric pushed his luck.

In secret, he'd been amassing allies. Most of them were Helen's family, but they had begun recruiting from the palace guard itself. There were many who had been forced into this life, many who wanted freedom from the mandates Blood Tristan laid upon them.

Despite the threat of a painful death for committing treason, many were willing to join his cause.

He kept an eye on Captain Alec, who had been thankfully sent off again to another isen Crusade. Helen would turn eighteen in less than two weeks, and the gossip mill of the palace—Cedric's most important source of information on the Blood and his activities— indicated certain promises had already been made about Helen's future.

Cedric did not have much time. He needed to recruit his small army and escape.

Someone knocked gently on the door, and the knob rattled. Three raps—the signal.

He stood and crossed to it, the door opening as he approached. Emmett stood in the hallway and nodded as their eyes met. Another soldier with a bald head and broad shoulders, Reed, leaned against the wall a short way off, eyes trained on the floor as Cedric emerged.

Emmett took off at a brisk pace in the opposite direction, and Cedric kept pace.

They stole through darkened hallways as stone floors became hardwood, careful to keep to the edges so as not to hit any of the squeaky boards and alert anyone in any of the rooms to their presence. As they hurried down a spiral staircase, Cedric caught a view of the thin sliver of the moon in the sky. Down below, no one walked through the empty streets. The lamps were out, and anyone unlucky enough to be outside would have to navigate by nothing more than starlight.

That was the plan: stay out of sight. Something Cedric, with his knack for bumping into walls and scuffling his boots on the floor, struggled to do. He sometimes wondered why he hadn't inherited the Hillsidians' natural stealth but imagined it had something to do with whatever Stone had done to him as a child.

Emmett held up a hand, eyes scanning the hallway. The abandoned stretch of the castle held its breath, painfully quiet. Still, Emmett kept his voice to a low grumble. "Before we go …"

"What is it?" Cedric whispered, also eyeing the stairwell nervously.

"A few things. For starters, you will be killed the moment you finish the last lichgate. I heard an order for your capture and, well, I believe Blood Tristan called it your dissection. They want to study you."

Cedric gulped. "Lovely."

Emmett frowned. "There's more."

"Of course, there is."

With a sigh, Emmett nodded. "Our time's up. Captain Alec made a formal request for Helen's hand. She turns eighteen soon, so my father can't hold them off any longer. Captain Alec made a—well, he made it clear to me what his intentions are a long time ago, but he has more confidence about it now and isn't trying to impress Father anymore. We need to get her out of the city as soon as possible."

Cedric cursed under his breath. "It certainly puts the squeeze on the timeline, but we don't have any choice, do we?"

Emmett shook his head. "Can you do it?"

Cedric shrugged. "I'll have to come up with something."

"Let's go."

Over the past few months, Emmett had begun to teach him stealth, and though Cedric wasn't exactly the best student, he had begun to pick it up. He followed the soldier on the balls of his feet, careful to tense his core and back as they stole through the night. It allowed him to at least keep up, despite his lack of bulk compared to his bear of a best friend.

Though the castle hallways bled together, each more identical than the last, Emmett eventually led him to a side door in the castle. As expected, no guard stood on duty as they slipped out to the cobblestone path leading away from the castle into the city.

It helped to have friends in the royal guard.

Together, he and Emmett darted through the darkness, keeping to the shadows and barely making a breath. The Hillsidian guard navigated the streets with ease, and Cedric kept close. Each time they did this, Emmett took him on a different route to be safe. While it meant they wouldn't be followed, their plan had the risk of Cedric getting lost the moment he stopped to catch his breath. Though Emmett had drawn him a map, there were no street names. No real landmarks aside from the occasional blue, front door.

To be honest, Cedric had no idea how Hillsidians navigated the city at all.

To make matters worse, Cedric had never had a chance to learn the city in more detail than Emmett's simple map, since he'd never been allowed to explore it. Every day he left, he marched to the lichgates surrounded by soldiers, many of whom he didn't trust. And every day, they ushered him back to his room. No exploration. No travel. Nothing new, day in and day out.

It would always be that way. As Stone had predicted, Blood Tristan regarded him as a threat—the man with no master was a threat to the person who relied on his people for his power.

The day Cedric had come here, he'd lost his freedom. And if he wanted it, he would have to take it back.

With a glance around the dark and empty street, Emmett slid up to one of the houses. A lone candle burned in the window, its flickering flame casting a pale glow on the windowsill. Hand balled into a fist, he rammed it against the door four times. The curtains in the window nearby rustled, brushing up against the glass, but no face appeared to greet them.

For a moment, nothing happened. The door didn't open. No voices came from inside. Cedric shifted his weight, glancing around the empty street. A terrified knot in his throat, he kept waiting for someone to appear on the corner. Anxious, ready to get this over with, he wished someone would open the door already.

The door cracked open, and a thin ray of yellow light stretched along the stoop and onto the street. Emmett pushed his way in, opening the door only enough to get by, and Cedric followed suit.

Inside, the hallway opened to a kitchen off to the right, where a gap in the window curtains revealed a hint of the flickering candlelight. A frail, elderly woman leaned against the doorframe and smiled widely as Cedric entered. Miss Ellie, Helen's grandmother. She wrapped him in a hug, pulling a bit on his shoulders as he stooped to return it, and she gestured for Emmett to join them.

"How are my boys?" She patted Cedric's back.

"Very well, thank you," he said.

Light chatter filtered from around the corner, and he followed it to find the living room and dining room both overflowing with people. He counted at least fifty. They huddled close, voices hushed, brows furrowed as many debated things he couldn't quite make out thanks to the whispering. A few of the younger members sat along the stairs, legs sticking through the gaps in the railing. A young man, only three or four years younger than Cedric, waved and grinned broadly as he entered. Cedric gave him a nod and a slight smile in return.

"Who do we have guarding the basement?" Cedric asked Emmett.

"Summers, Anders, and Ryker. No one's getting up from the tunnels."

Cedric let out a slow breath of relief. Over time, he had learned about the endless labyrinth of tunnels beneath Hillside that connected to most of the houses in the capital city. They had been created to offer an escape if the city were ever attacked, and for those who knew the way, they all lead to the castle itself. These routes were heavily guarded at all times, and voices carried in the stone tunnels. Cedric didn't want to take any chances, and any time they were in a house connected to the labyrinth, he posted guard.

"They're here!" someone said from the back of the living room.

As if on cue, the voices hushed. No one spoke, and every head turned toward Cedric.

He hated this part.

True, to be a leader meant people would listen, but his throat always went dry the moment every eye trained on him. Thanks to a life in the forest with Stone, he wasn't used to spotlight. He wasn't used to attention, and he certainly wasn't used to telling people what to do.

He tensed his jaw, squaring his shoulders as he tried to tune the people out. He had to focus. He pretended he was back in the forest with Stone, talking to his mentor in the humming stillness of the woods.

Soft fingers wove through his, and he turned his head to find Helen standing next to him, offering him a sweet smile. A thin trickle of relief rushed through him, and he stood a little taller with her by his side.

He returned his attention to the crowd gathered throughout Miss Ellie's living room. "Thank you for being here. I know it's dangerous for you to come, but these meetings, when we can have them, are so important. We have new vagabonds joining us today, and it's important for you to meet them so you know who's safe to talk to and who is not. Would those who are joining us today please come forward?"

Six men stepped forward in the crowd, stopping before Cedric and standing with their hands behind their backs. Each wore the green and gold uniforms of the palace guard, and Cedric found himself staring up at each of them. They were massive soldiers, muscular and trained for war.

It was exactly what he'd ask for.

"Thank you for this honor," the tallest said.

Cedric nodded, not quite ready to welcome them into the ranks. "Why do you want to join us?"

The guard lifted his chin, staring at the wall as he spoke as though he were being drilled by a sergeant. "I've dreamed of freedom my whole life. I never wanted to be a soldier, but I was drafted at fifteen because of my physical ability. I've been in the elite guard ever since I completed my training, and I've seen the Blood and the motivations behind the decisions he makes. It worries me that we must obey such a militant man, and I'm not interested in doing it any longer."

The guard next to him grunted in agreement. "We're all in the same unit, and we all believe the same thing. We want out."

Cedric considered what they'd said. He could understand, but their freedom would mean more war. "Keep in mind, this isn't just about Hillside. This isn't about breaking down Blood Tristan and making him do what we think is right. It's about uniting all of the kingdoms and convincing them to support peace and gentle ruling. Yakona need their Bloods, and the Bloods need their yakona. Our fight is about bringing balance back to the kingdoms. This won't be a war if I can help it, but more of a chance for the Bloods to remember they serve us as much as we serve them. When people learn about us, because it's inevitable that it will happen, many will try to kill us. This is not a brotherhood to be entered lightly, and I need to know you're ready for bloodshed if it comes."

The six guards stood a little straighter, each of them with their eyes trained on his. They nodded in unison.

"We're ready," the tallest said.

Satisfied and a bit grateful, Cedric took a deep breath and gestured for the stairs. "Then let's not waste any time."

CHAPTER TWELVE

AGE 19

Late Autumn
The Kingdom of Hillside

An hour later, Cedric groaned and sank down a wall in the upstairs hallway, stretching his legs as he sat on the floor and rubbed his eyes. Thanks to his late-night escapades, he didn't sleep much anymore.

The gentle chatter of his vagabonds drifted up the stairs, and he smiled. They were worth every sleepless night.

The six guards had spread across the three bedrooms on this floor of the house, each taking a bed. He'd successfully turned them all, raising their energy levels until they severed their connections with Blood

Tristan. But silently, without asking, Cedric had also looked at each of their most influential memories. It was a gift he'd kept to himself, even from Helen. He didn't expect she'd like him prying into the minds of her closest family and friends, but he had to know what motivated each one to join his cause. He had to be certain. And though a twinge of guilt accompanied each reading, he had yet to feel the need to stop.

Deep down, he dreaded the moment he feared most —finding a traitor, finding someone who came simply to betray them. He had the ability to kill them. With an additional turn of the gem, he could end their lives and protect his vagabonds. Though he dreaded ever facing the choice, he knew he didn't have one.

It would have to be done.

Ronan, the last guard he'd worked on tonight had been recruited to the soldier Academy at age nine. The thought churned Cedric's stomach, and his face flushed with nausea at the thought of a child wielding a sword. His mother had wept openly on the doorstep as Blood Tristan's soldiers had pulled him away, and as a child, Ronan hadn't been able to understand what was happening. He thought he'd done something wrong, begged his mother to forgive him. He hadn't been allowed home since, and he had received a letter last week that his mother died. He hadn't even been allowed to leave to attend her memorial.

Cedric shook his head, disgusted. Blood Tristan had lost touch with his subjects, provided he'd ever had the compassion to begin with. The people in his kingdom seemed to be nothing more than minions to him, objects that fulfilled his needs and could be controlled if they rebelled.

It would take a miracle to change such thinking. After all, changing the Blood's mind was his only option.

The stairs creaked, and Helen's striking face appeared over the top most stair. The honey-sweet aroma of roses radiated from her, floating before her like an invisible mist. She grinned and tilted her head slightly in welcome, and his eyes were drawn to the slender slope of her neck and the curve of her shoulders as they appeared. He resisted the impulse to look lower, careful to keep his eyes on hers. A wave of desire rushed through him, and he waited quietly, relishing her like he would a breath of fresh air.

"Hello, stranger," she said, kissing him on the cheek as she sat beside him.

"Hello, mischief," he said with a grin.

She laughed, the sound like birds singing. He set his arm around her and pulled her close, thumb rubbing her shoulder as she leaned her head against his.

With her finger, she drew circles on his chest. "How did it go?"

He swallowed hard, distracted by her touch and half-wishing he could lead her into one of the bedrooms. Despite her almost nightly visits, he had never dared to take it further than playful kisses, not with her brother often outside the door. Cedric frowned. He sometimes wondered if she even wanted it.

It took him a moment to remember her question. "Turning the soldiers went well. I have faith in all of them. They'll be incredibly helpful."

"Good to hear. I was a little worried about them, since I don't know any of them personally. You've already changed everyone I can recommend."

He rubbed her arm. "And thank you. They all took on a lot of responsibility when they joined us, but I respect everyone you brought to our cause. I'm grateful you're here with me."

"Thanks for trusting me," she said, her eyes catching his.

A lock of her dark hair fell across her face, and he tucked it behind her ear. "There's no one else I would rather share this death wish with."

She laughed. "That's the spirit. So, what's next? More recruits?"

He shook his head. "Things are about to change, Helen. We need to go to the next stage."

"What do you mean?"

He ran his hand through his hair, frustrated. "You're

out of time. We have to get you out of the city before Captain Alec gets his way. Even though you don't have a blood loyalty anymore, Blood Tristan will still expect you to obey him. If you stay, you'll either be forced to bond with Captain Alec or exposed as a vagabond."

Her smile fell, and her grip on his arm tightened a bit. "You won't let it happen."

"Not a chance. That's why it's important I get you out of here."

"But how?"

He shrugged. "Great question. The only place I know to take you is likely still heavily watched. And what's more, when you and I disappear at the same time, Blood Tristan will put two and two together. He'll question or interrogate your entire family."

"Can't we bring them, too? All the vagabonds?"

"I don't see how. It's not easy to travel with nearly sixty yakona, much less stay hidden the entire trip. Hillside has the best trackers in all of Ourea. Blood Tristan will come after us, and we'll have to move quickly. It's better if we can send for them later, once we have somewhere to go. Those who remain behind are going to have to pretend they knew nothing about us."

"You don't think he would torture them, do you?"

Cedric slumped, tugging at the ends of his hair. "I hope not."

"I mean, Blood Tristan can be cruel, but that's too

far, even for him."

Cedric didn't have an answer. He didn't know.

"… Right?" she prodded.

"I wonder if we could just kill him," Cedric said without thinking.

Helen gasped, and he regretted what he'd said as soon as he said it. It wasn't his way to kill, not if he had other means. Getting rid of the bigot simply seemed like it would make things so much easier.

"If our Blood and Heir both die, every Hillsidian with the blood loyalty will die," she said.

Cedric sat up straighter, watching her as he tried to figure out if she was making a bad joke. But her eyes remained wide, her lips parted in genuine horror at the idea.

"But the prince—"

Helen shook her head. "There are rumors he doesn't have the bloodline. Some say he's not a true Heir. As far as we know, Blood Tristan is the only royal."

Cedric set his face in his hands, discouraged. Yet again, this complicated things. Killing a Blood who had no Heir would also kill his subjects, destroying the very people Cedric was trying to protect. Maybe even the vagabonds, as they still had something of a connection to the Blood, even if they were free to disobey.

This little tidbit seemed like something important enough for Stone to have mentioned at some point in Cedric's childhood, but important things often seem trivial to the isen. Cedric groaned, gritting his teeth. "I didn't know. I'm sorry."

"Just don't scare me like that," she said, setting a hand on her chest.

They sat in silence, staring at the wall as he listened to the quiet chatter below. Cedric heard occasional words: vagabond, freedom, his name. He had promised these people so much, and the weight of their expectations often kept him up long after he finally did have a chance to sleep.

He tapped his finger on the floor, deep in thought. "All right, so think about what we need. We need a safe place for everyone to gather outside of the capital where the Blood can't kill us at any minute. We need our own space, a safe, self-sustaining village where we can grow in numbers."

"Does that exist? Is there some neutral village we can go to?"

Cedric shook his head. "We'll have to make it. Stone should be able to help us with that, so the next course of action is to go to him. When we leave, that's where we'll need to go."

"When do we leave?"

"What if we left tonight? You, me, and Emmett. No

more. We tell Reed to let his superiors think Emmett took over guarding my room for the evening. It should be enough to protect him and keep him in their good graces. We'll find and stay with my mentor." He paused, eyes on the floor, wondering if this new idea was too brazen. Too sudden.

Too stupid.

After all, Stone was an isen—a fact no one else knew. He didn't know how he could tell them. Helen and her family had grown up in Hillside, a kingdom famous for its isen hunters. Hatred for isen was bred into them.

And yet, he had no other options.

"You want us to leave tonight?" Helen sat up straighter, a finger tapping her lip as her eyes slipped out of focus.

Cedric nodded, growing fonder of his plan the more it swirled around in his brain. He'd taken to stowing his book and the white gem in a false floor-board of Miss Ellie's house, and they were the only possessions he owned. He didn't even need to go back to his cell. "Originally, I was going to ask Blood Tristan to let me leave. I was going to try to get on his good graces before I left, but I don't think there's a point. I'll leave a note with the instructions on how they can finish their lichgates, but I don't think we can be here anymore. Blood Tristan could kill me any day, and he could order you to bond with Captain Alec at any moment. There's no reason for us to stay."

Helen's gaze drifted to the stairs as the vagabonds' gentle chatter filled the silence. "There are plenty of reasons for us to stay."

He held her hands. For a moment, he lost himself in her dark eyes. "Helen, they will join us. Once we have a safe place for them to live, we'll give them maps to find us. They'll say they're visiting family in the outer villages, and one by one, they'll come to us. They'll be safe. But you? Me? We're not."

She nodded, her grip tightening on his hands. "I know. I was just—no, you're right. You're absolutely right. We need to go, and we need to go now."

He leaned his forehead against hers, and he wished he could say something inspiring. Something to encourage her, to let her know that he would be there for her to matter what happened. But nothing came, and he settled with a simple question. "Are you ready for this?"

She smiled, that mischievous twinkle back in her eyes. "With you looking out for me, I'm ready for anything."

I t took about two hours to get food and supplies together, brief the rest of the vagabonds, and prepare to leave. Cedric handed a note to one of the vagabonds who worked in the palace kitchens—instructions on how to complete a lichgate, which she would leave on his bed for the morning guards to find. And while she was there, she would warn Reed of what was coming and what to say.

Cedric waited by the front door, a pack over one shoulder as he watched Helen pull her father into a deep hug. Their eyes closed, sad smiles on their faces, and they held each other. No words passed between them, but it seemed as though they didn't need to speak to express everything they needed to say. They were showing their love for each other, the sadness of how much they would miss each other, the fear they would never see each other again—all of it passed between them without a word, and even he could feel it.

He cracked his knuckles to distract himself from thoughts of Stone, the not-father who could never have feelings, much less miss him.

"We should get going," Emmett said. He stood in the kitchen with one arm around Miss Ellie and heavy backpack loaded on his shoulders.

Helen nodded, and she smiled one last time at her father. "You all be safe, now. Lay low."

"You, too," her father said.

"We'll send word as soon as we have a safe place for you all to join us," Cedric said, his hand on the doorknob.

"You take care of her," her father said.

"I will, sir. I promise." Cedric bowed his head in respect, and Emmett open the door to the basement cellar. The three of them hurried down the stairs and into the tunnels below the house.

As the door shut behind them, Cedric nudged Emmett. "You're sure there's a lichgate down here we can use?"

The soldier nodded. "It's punishment duty. When you do something stupid, you get stuck guarding this lichgate. It's deep in the tunnels, difficult to get to, and it takes half an hour just to show up for your shift after such a walk. It leads to an open field where you can see for miles. It's nothing but short grass as far as the eye can see. If any attackers were ever coming, the soldier would know long before they came. Even if they got through, the attackers would get lost and starve to death in the labyrinth beneath the city. Strategically, it's of little threat, so the worst performers are put on duty."

"Do you know how to get to Endervere from there?"

Emmett shook his head. "I don't. However, I do know there's a village about a day's walk from the lichgate. We can probably get directions there and leave before anyone realizes who we are or what were up to. We'll have to ask for directions to several cities to throw them off our scent."

"But the Blood knows I'm from Endervere. He found me there."

"And what idiot would go back to the one place his Blood suspected he would go?" Emmett grinned.

"We're relying on the Blood to assume I'm too smart to go back?"

"Exactly."

Helen laughed. Cedric grinned, shaking his head as he hoped against hope this would work.

The stony tunnels went on for ages, and all Cedric could think about were the hours ticking down until the guards shifted and someone realized he was missing from his cell. Hopefully, by now, the vagabonds had returned to their homes. His disappearance would start a mad hunt for accomplices, and he needed all of them to stay safe.

After at least an hour, Emmett paused at a sharp bend in the hall and lifted his hand to stop them. Cedric stopped short, pressing his back against the wall for cover. Helen leaned against him, the soft skin of her arm brushing against his. He leaned into her on impulse, his instinct always to keep her close.

"I'll be right back," Emmett whispered. He walked

around the corner, his footsteps thumping on the stone floor.

"First Lieutenant Morris, what a surprise!" a young man said out of view, his voice trembling.

"Slouching and sleeping on the job again. I can't say I'm shocked, unfortunately," Emmett said, his voice carrying a harsher tone than Cedric was used to.

Helen chuckled softly. "Everyone in the palace thinks he's terrifying, but it's really just a teddy bear."

"Maybe to you," Cedric said under his breath, grinning.

She shrugged.

"Get back to base, soldier!" Emmett ordered.

"B-but I still have two hours on—"

"That's an order!"

"Sir! Yes, sir!" Boots skidded over the stone floor, their thumping growing louder as whomever was on duty neared. Panicked, Cedric tilted his body to hide Helen from view as best he could.

"Not that way, idiot," Emmett snapped.

"B-but sir, it's the fastest—"

"Did I say you could take the quick route? Head southeast, and I order you to run the whole way. Go!"

"Sir, yes sir!" The footsteps retreated, and the huffing wheeze of someone struggling to breathe disappeared down the hallway.

Cedric waited, ears straining as he listened to the soldier's feet slap along the stone. The man's wheezing gasps for air left Cedric feeling a bit out of breath himself.

Emmett appeared around the corner and gestured for them to hurry. Cedric obeyed and, holding Helen's hand, they ran into the hallway. It was as bare as the rest of the hallways had been except for the lichgate on the far wall—a slender archway of dried, old vines grown into the rock. Beyond the portal, the muted landscape of a grassy meadow swayed in a breeze that didn't reach the stagnant tunnel. A starry night stretched on forever above the field, tempting Cedric toward freedom.

With a stern glance over the tunnel, Emmett ushered Cedric in first. He hurried through. As he passed, the familiar kick to his gut and the blast of blue light in the corner of his eye reminded him of all the work he'd been doing on the Blood's lichgates. He grinned, grateful that part of his life was over.

His smile fell, however, when he imagined Blood Tristan's fury at finding the note. Without a doubt, the entire kingdom of Hillside would be after him soon. And not just him, but Helen and Emmett as well. They had to get as far away as they could, as quickly as possible.

The tall grasses tickled his fingers as he stood in the meadow, drinking in the midnight sky. Thousands of stars glittered overhead like twinkling gems sewn into a black blanket. The faintest, blue glow emanated from the field, allowing the barest amount of light to lead them through the field. Helen joined him, smiling as she took in the landscape at his side.

"It's beautiful," she said.

He smiled without looking away from her. "It is."

"Enough of that," Emmett said, snapping his fingers. He jogged through the grass and gestured for them to follow. Cedric kept pace as best he could, and Helen ran easily beside him.

They had a long way to go, and not much time to make it there.

CHAPTER THIRTEEN

AGE 19

Late Autumn
Endervere, Kingdom of Hillside

A fter their quick stop in the village to ask for directions, it took a week of sleeping in the trees, each taking turns as a lookout, to reach Endervere. As the sun set on their seventh day in the wilderness, Cedric finally knelt behind the brush along the edge of town, his eyes drooping from the exhaustion of traveling through dark forests to remain unseen and a knot of nerves forming in his throat. Shoulders tense, stomach rumbling, he ducked behind a large oak by the road into town. Helen and Emmett followed, each taking cover behind a nearby trunk.

Two soldiers in the green and gold uniforms of the castle guard patrolled the path, kicking clouds of dust into the air as they strolled the dirt road into town. Familiar, brown buildings framed the town square, and from his vantage point, Cedric caught the elbow of the Blood's statue in the center of the village.

After all those days and months in his cell at the palace, he thought for sure he would never see it again.

Cedric peeked around the tree, eager to get a count on the military presence in his hometown. More men in green tunics lined with gold along the hem wandered through the alleys. It seemed as though every second, he caught sight of a golden helmet here, a pair of heads there. Too many patrols, not enough civilians. One soldier held his sword in the light of a nearby street lamp, it's light glinting off the steel, and he ran his thumb along it.

Nails biting into the bark of the tree, Cedric tensed his jaw and gestured for Emmett to come closer. They needed a strategy.

"These guys are bad news," Emmett said under his breath while shuffling closer.

Helen leaned in, the bush's leaves trembling as she joined them. "What makes these guys so bad?"

Emmett shook his head. "Look at the red marks on their tunics. They're a special unit. Brutal killers. Trained to take no prisoners. The problem soldiers end up in this unit, and they're sent wherever the warring is worst. Now, this could mean a few different things. Option one: isen or another yakona kingdom has attacked here recently. Or, option two: Blood Tristan isn't happy with how Endervere civilians have been behaving."

"I vote option two," Cedric said dryly.

"They're probably looking for us," Helen said.

Emmett nudged Cedric's shoulder. "Are we close to the safe house?"

"Very."

"And you're sure no one has found it?"

"Not a chance." Cedric had no doubt Stone's hideaway would be secure. Not even the boys playing in the woods ever stumbled across them by accident. Thanks to whatever charms and protections Stone had placed around the house, it wouldn't be discovered.

"Then let's keep going." Emmett cracked his neck.

Cedric pointed off into the woods toward a familiar deer trail. He sometimes took this route when he wanted a change of scenery, so he could still navigate to the house from here. "Stone's home is this way. Come on."

A twinge of guilt burned through him. He still hadn't had the courage to tell them what Stone was. He needed them to meet him first, to see he was harmless before—

"You see that?" One of the guards along the road nudged his companion and pointed toward them.

"Yeah, the leaves moved." The other soldier drew his sword and took a step closer.

"Hurry, they're moving this way," Emmett said.

Cedric grimaced and hurried through the under-brush, careful to stick to the deer trail and keep themselves low as they ran. Behind them, Emmett would stop occasionally to pat the ground, to veer off and break a twig somewhere else, all to throw any trackers off their scent. He'd been doing this the entire trek, and Cedric was grateful to have such an elite soldier with them. He didn't know how he and Helen would have managed otherwise.

Still, he scanned the forest as they hurried along the deer trail, terrified one of the guards had either heard them or would happen by.

Forty, tense, minutes passed as they raced through the woods. Cedric's back ached, his legs screamed for a moment's rest, and he had a headache he knew could only be cured with water and sleep. But with each step he took toward his childhood home, he felt stronger. More energized. More ready and capable of taking on the world. He pressed on, eager to get them to safety.

At least—as safe as they could be as fugitives from the Hillsidian Blood. Stone wasn't exactly the most accommodating of hosts, himself.

Finally, a familiar pair of trees appeared around a bend in the path. The trunks of the two oaks bent toward each other to form an archway, and through them was a diluted, wooden door with a brass knob.

Cedric smiled, grateful to have found one of the lich-gates that served as a door into his childhood house.

Each step brought him more energy. With a broad smile, Cedric reached through the lichgate and ripped open the door as a kick in his stomach warned him he'd passed through the portal. A familiar flash of blue light rippled along his periphery as he entered the house. He left the door open and set his hands on his hips as he took in the familiar staircase, the fireplace, the kitchen.

Home.

"Well it's about time," Stone said. The isen sat at the dining table to the right of the door, one leg crossed as he sipped a cup of tea.

What a lovely welcome.

"It's great to see you, too," Cedric said, suppressing the urge to roll his eyes.

Helen entered behind him, and Emmett behind her. The soldier slammed the door shut and cracked his neck, sighing with relief as he dropped his pack to the floor. "Famished. Anything to eat?"

Stone eyed the pair for a moment, unmoving, one brow quirked in annoyance. "Company. Marvelous."

"Stone, these are—"

"Yes, yes, it's fine. There's dried meats and bread in the pantry." Stone stood and walked toward the stairwell.

Helen frowned. "Stone? But you don't look like the man in the—"

"I'm an isen, child," Stone said, passing her on his way to the stairwell.

"An isen!" Helen and Emmett shouted in unison. Emmett shoved Helen aside, putting himself between her and Stone. He drew his sword, its tip pointing at the isen's throat.

Spectacular.

Cedric rubbed his face. This was one detail that hadn't gone according to plan. There had never been a real moment to tell them the truth, not in a way they'd understand. He'd wanted them to get to know Stone first, but of course the old fart had to go and ruin it.

"Nice job," Cedric said, balling his hand into a fist as he glared at his not-father.

Stone shrugged. "Feed them and get on with whatever you're up to. I'm going to bed."

The isen disappeared up the stairs. Both Helen and Emmett, however, turned their fury on Cedric.

"You knew he was an isen?" Emmett demanded, sword thankfully pointed at the floor.

"You let an isen change me?" Helen crossed her arms, fuming.

Emmett gritted his teeth. "Cedric, I'll kill you if that's true. You're supposed to protect her. How can you say you love her when—"

"Relax. Enough! Stop." Cedric lifted his hands in surrender.

"Explain. Right now," Helen snapped.

Cedric licked his lips, wondering how in Ourea he was going to get them to come around to the idea of trusting their kingdom's greatest enemy. "I realize this is difficult to understand or accept, but Stone raised me since I was a child. He's the one who broke my blood loyalty, and he's the one who taught me how to break yours. He's not a threat to us. He's our most valuable ally, and he can help us find a place to make our own. We need him, so please, put aside your hatred for isen long enough to accept his help."

"Isen are evil creatures and not to be trusted!" Emmett gestured toward the stairwell.

"Then why didn't he kill me when I was a baby?" Cedric asked.

Though Emmett still fumed, Helen's shoulders relaxed a bit.

"How about when I was older? Stronger? More useful? If Blood Tristan and the isen hunters are right, if isen are opportunistic killers with no basic decency, why did Stone let me live? Why did he raise me? Feed me? Teach me? Everything I know, I know because of him. That isen up there. He's an ass, but he's not evil."

"I heard that," Stone said from upstairs.

Cedric ignored his not-father, focusing instead on the two Hillsidians between him and the door. Emmett tightened his grip on his sword handle, the strain of skin on metal almost deafening. He scowled, creases along his mouth as he no doubt debated his options.

Helen, however, stared at the floor. Her eyes eventually wandered across the walls of the small home. "You're right."

Relieved, Cedric let out a slow breath. "Really? You understand?"

She nodded. "He raised you. He could have left you for dead or stolen your soul when you were older. But he didn't. And he didn't hurt me, either."

Cedric breathed a sigh of relief and set his hands on his head. "Right, exactly. He didn't. He came to Hillside, helped me while I was trapped there. I never would have locked the lichgate without his help."

Emmett's mouth dropped open. "*Bloods,* he was in Hillside? An isen! In Hillside!"

"And it was fine. No mass murder. No panic," Cedric added.

Helen shook her head. "You still lied to me. To all of us."

Cedric rubbed his neck, unable to look her in the eye. "I know, and I'm sorry. I trust you two most in the world, with almost anything, but I didn't tell you this because I knew even you two would react with hatred. I didn't think you would value what he can do for us. Yes, he's an isen, and there's a lot of hate between his kind and yakona. I needed you to meet him first. I wanted you to see he's not a threat. Please, forgive me."

Out of words, he finally caught her eye, pleading with her through his expression, through his outstretched hands. She didn't reach for him, instead watching him out of the corner of her eye, back arched and arms crossed as if she were deciding his fate. In many ways, she was. She was about to decide if this was it, if this was a lie that would break her trust in him.

He swallowed hard, awaiting her decision.

She sighed. "I understand. But Cedric, you can never lie to me like this again I don't care what your reason is. Do you understand? You tell me everything. Always."

He nodded and resisted the impulse to pull her into a deep kiss. "Thank you."

She rubbed her eyes. "Is it safe to sleep here? We all need some rest."

"You two sleep. I'll keep watch." Emmett sat at the dining room table, back to the wall as he faced the stairwell, glaring at it with all his might.

"Emmett, I'm sorry," Cedric said.

The soldier snapped his fingers and pointed to the stairs. "I'm in no mood to deal with you right now. Go to bed."

With a sigh, Cedric obeyed, gently brushing his fingers along Helen's shoulder as he passed. She followed close behind, and the stairs creaked with each footstep.

"There's only one bed, so I can sleep on the floor," Cedric said, heart racing despite his exhaustion at the thought of her asleep in his room.

"I don't know how safe I feel with an isen down the hall from me. You should sleep in the bed with me, between me and the door."

He arched his back on impulse, and it took all his self-control to resist the stupid grin that so desperately wanted to spread across his lips. "If you insist."

She laughed. "You're shameless. You're not out of trouble yet, Cedric. Don't you try anything tonight, not even a kiss."

He relaxed his shoulders, a bit defeated, but it was a fair point. He'd have to earn his way back into her good graces. For now, he relished his small triumph. He'd escaped Blood Tristan, made it to Stone's house, and was finally on track to establish a safe haven for his vagabonds.

His only problem: where in all of Ourea would he find a place safe enough for the yakona who would become traitors of every kingdom if they were discovered?

CHAPTER FOURTEEN

AGE 19

Late Autumn
Childhood Home

The next morning, Cedric woke to a blinding beam of sunlight. He squinted, blinking rapidly as he cleared the spots from his vision and sat up in bed. Orange rays burst through the glass panes in the wall of his small, childhood bedroom. Only his bed filled the otherwise empty space, the plain wooden panels along the wall matching those in the floor. Dust floated in the light, churning as a gust blew through the open window.

He'd intended to talk with Helen long into the night, to wake up late and let himself have one evening of peace, but he had fallen asleep the moment his head hit the pillow. He rubbed his face, eyes stinging.

Though his head ached, and he wanted to sleep more, energy pumped through his body. His muscles were looser, his mood better, and his hope restored. It was as if being in his childhood home had washed away his years in the Hillsidian capital and given him renewed vigor.

Helen lay next to him, arms curled around the pillow as her dark hair cascaded over her shoulders. She smiled in her sleep, breathing rhythmically beneath his comforter.

He wanted to reach out and touch her, to run his hand along her cheek, but he didn't want to wake her. She hadn't slept much lately, and he doubted she was used to sleep deprivation from life on the run. He would let her rest.

Cedric stood and slipped out of his room, careful to keep to the edges of the stairs so as not to let them creak. But as he reached the foot of the stairwell, he found a scowling Emmett staring at him, arms crossed. The hulking man still sat at the dinner table, ankle resting on his knee. His frown deepened as their eyes met.

Ah. Of course. They hadn't quite resolved the whole isen issue last night.

"Good morning," Cedric said, nervously running a hand through his hair.

Emmett's eyes narrowed. He said nothing.

Cedric drank in the scene: bread crumbs on a plate,

squared shoulders, bags beneath the soldier's eyes. "Did you sleep at all?"

"Not with an isen and a liar in the house."

Cedric huffed in frustration. "Technically, I didn't lie. I omitted important information."

"There's no difference!"

Not in an altogether forgiving mood, Cedric arched his back and frowned. "There's a world of difference. I did what I had to do to get us out of Hillside and find someplace safe. I grew up here, I know Stone, and he won't hurt either of you. You're my friends, and even though Stone has—you could say—dubious morals, he's not going to do anything to you. You can relax, and while you're at it, let it go. I've apologized for not telling you about Stone, and I explained why I acted this way. You were raised to hate isen without bothering to learn more about them, and I knew you would react this way. But he's our only ally outside of Hillside, and we need him. I did what I had to do, and you're smart enough to understand why I did what I did. Do you trust me or not?"

Emmett tightened his fist, a muscle popping like a cracked knuckle as a vain appeared in his brow. Cedric suppressed the impulse to cringe and prepare himself for the wave of anger that would inevitably come, but he'd meant every word he said. This was the moment, Emmett's opportunity to either trust Cedric or leave. Terror clawed at Cedric's gut as he waited for his friend to speak, afraid of what he would say or do, but simultaneously eager to get it over with. To move on.

The vagabonds back in Hillside depended on them, and they didn't have time for squabbles or prejudice.

With a slow breath, Emmett stretched his fingers out on the table and sighed. "You're right."

Cedric flinched in surprise. "I don't think I've ever heard you use those words."

Emmett chuckled and shook his head, running his hands through his hair. "Don't get me wrong, I'm still furious. I detest isen. They steal souls and enslave yakona, stealing their magic and preventing them from dying properly. It's not a fate I'd wish on anyone, and I still think any creature capable of such evil should be destroyed. I've been trained to hunt them since I could hold a sword. I've seen what they can do, Cedric. Mine is a deep hatred, and it's not going to be solved by spending the night in an isen's house. So yes, I can understand why you didn't tell me."

Cedric sighed with relief. "So glad—"

"However," Emmett interrupted, "I don't care how you think I'll act, or what you think I'll do. You will keep me informed of all future decisions, especially ones involving isen. I didn't get where I am by operating on blind faith. I trusted you thus far because I believe in what you're doing. What we're doing. We're a team, Cedric. I gave up everything to join your cause —my career, my home, my entire world. And I did it because I believe changing Ourea is my purpose. I'm here to fight. And while I'm grateful you gave me my freedom from Blood Tristan, I'm not just going to obediently follow you out of gratitude. My loyalty is earned. Do you understand?"

The muscles in Cedric's jaw tensed, and he nodded. "Understood."

Emmett eyed Cedric up and down. "And you better have slept on the floor."

Before he could help it, a blush crept up Cedric's neck. He cleared his throat and mumbled under his breath, hoping Emmett would take it as an answer.

Someone coughed in the kitchen, and Cedric twisted his head toward the welcome distraction. Stone leaned against the wall, holding a clay mug with steam radiating from the top. The isen quirked an eyebrow. "Have you ladies reconciled?"

Emmett stared at Stone, his scowl returning and fists once more tightening. The imposing soldier hardened almost like a statue, and Cedric impulsively took the reins of the conversation to keep the peace. "Good morning, Stone."

"Hmph." Stone sat at the head of the table, opposite Emmett, despite the hatred radiating from the soldier like an aura. His not-father had never been one for small talk or pleasantries, but it been the first thing Cedric could think of.

Despite his entire childhood of living under what

could generously be called Stone's "care," spending time with Stone again after the years of kindness and warmth from Helen's family would take some getting used to.

"Tell me why you came all the way out here with two strangers," Stone said, sipping his drink.

"I've turned more vagabonds, and I need—"

"I still don't know why you're bothering with this." Stone shook his head.

Cedric grimaced. "I told you before you left that this is important to me."

"Yes, but why?"

"Because I have a responsibility—"

"No, you don't."

Emmett huffed, leaning back in his chair crossing his arms. Cedric followed suit, leaning against the wall by the stairs, doing his best to suppress the annoyance bubbling in his gut. "Stone, I can defy my Blood. It's a gift. This gift can help others. This gift can change the world. We can change the way the Bloods treat their subjects. We can make Ourea a better place, and I would be selfish to ignore those who need me."

"Why should you live your life for someone else? Simply live it. You don't owe anyone anything. Not even me."

"I can't do that. I can't live like you. I need purpose, direction, something to do. I need—"

"You don't need to put your life on the line."

"I'm trying—"

"You're young and you're foolish. You're gifted. Don't trap yourself into—"

Cedric slammed his fist against the wall. "I'm not gifted. I'm nothing more than another of your experiments!"

Silence followed. Emmett stared at him, eyes wide and his scowl replaced with a blank look of surprise. Stone, meanwhile, raised an eyebrow.

But the dam had burst, and Cedric couldn't stop. "I'm nothing more than an experiment, Stone. Just another creature you broke when I was too young and powerless to defend myself. And what's more, I think I'm a *failed* experiment. You made a mistake, and you kept me around to monitor my progress, to see what the effects would be. But if I'm nothing more than a mistake, I may as well use whatever you did to me to make the world a little better. That's why I'm *bothering* with this, and even if I don't owe you anything, you owe me this favor!"

Cedric set his hands on his head, sucking in deep breaths as he turned his back to the table and tried to calm himself. He tugged on the roots of his hair, willing his anger to subside. In the moment of silence that followed, his heart settled, and his breath slowed.

"So, what is it you need?" Stone asked calmly.

Cedric rubbed his eyes, still refusing to turn around. His outburst had led to victory, sure, but a tainted one. "A place for all my vagabonds to live safely, out of the watchful eye of the Blood. A place where we can be safe."

Neither Stone nor Emmett spoke. A floorboard creaked, and a gust of wind hit the side of the house, shooting shivers down the wooden walls. Cedric turned around to see his not-father staring at the floor, eyes out of focus, no doubt debating options. This would be another challenge, and Stone seemed to apply the same mild interest he gave any experiment.

Cedric grimaced in disgust.

Stone tapped his finger on the table. "The location of your new vagabond village should have at least one lichgate to give you direct access to this house. You'll need a space away from everyone to relax and regain your vigor."

Cedric didn't reply, but Stone's choice of words struck him as odd. It was a confirmation of what he'd felt this morning, of the energy and strength he drew from these walls. In some way, Cedric was connected to the house, and he wouldn't bother asking how. He had no faith he would get an answer, much less one he would like.

Stone stood, only a faint trail of steam still emanating from the mug he abandoned on the table. "What else?"

"We need a way to protect our little city," Emmett grumbled. Cedric could only imagine what the Hillsidian soldier was going through, allying with an isen. It must've been a serious affront to his pride.

"We need several layers of protection," Cedric added.

"Any preferences?" Stone paced about the living room, hands behind his back.

"A locked lichgate, similar to the one we made for Hillside, and preferably in a dangerous area. Someplace no yakona would ever want to go, even if they had a good reason to."

Stone nodded. "A good idea, I admit. The isen guild I stayed with did the same to protect their secret city, though they relied on rumors. The forest itself was harmless."

A low rumble emanated from Emmett's chest, and the scowl returned. He stretched his arms across the table, hunching in his chair as he stared at the ceiling with his hands balled into fists. Cedric could only imagine the battle raging between Emmett's instinct and self-control at hearing yet another reference to Stone's isen nature.

Cedric shook his head. This hatred would take a while to heal, it seemed. He rubbed his chin, losing himself to the task at hand to distract himself from his own anger and Emmett's. "The village also needs to be accessible. We can make this house one of the entrances."

Stone scoffed. "I don't need a bunch of strange people walking to my home. We'll find something else."

"I haven't seen enough of Ourea to have any other ideas."

"I'll think about it." Stone returned to his seat, chin on his fist as he stared out the window. His fingers tapped slowly against the table, and the last of the steam from his mug disappeared.

"We could—"

"Enough, I'm thinking." Stone waved him away with the flick of his wrist.

Cedric's eye twitched with annoyance, but he gritted his teeth to suppress another impulsive outburst.

How great to be home.

CHAPTER FIFTEEN

AGE 19

Late Autumn
Childhood Home

Throughout the entire day, Stone barely moved from his place at the table. Cedric, meanwhile, quickly gave up on watching his not-father sit and think. He retreated outside with the notebook Stone had given him back in Hillside, hell-bent on distracting himself from the anger still stewing within him.

As the sun shifted beyond the dense canopy above, Cedric quickly lost track of time. He spent his day staring into the wood, wondering if he was doing the right thing, wondering if he was in over his head after all. Wondering, with disgust and anger, if Stone was right. If this was a mistake. If he had started something he would never be able to finish.

The notebook sat open at his side, a ladybug crawling across the paper, a clean quill resting in the grass beside an inkwell. He felt compelled to write, to spill his thoughts until they started making sense, until he could find something concrete among the fear and anxiety, but his eyes always shifted out of focus before he drummed up the will to put anything on paper.

Finally, he picked up the book and laid it in his lap, thinking about how he'd gotten here in the first place. His mind wandered back to meeting the Blood for the first time, to being chained and thrown in jail, to escaping experimentation and certain death with his wit alone. He had locked a lichgate, escaped the Blood, and started a revolution. He had freed guards and civilians alike, and each of these vagabonds were dedicated to spreading freedom and balance within the yakona world.

And he, of all people, had set this in motion.

A patch of clover to his right shivered in a light breeze, and he studied the pedals. A four-leaf clover stood out above the patch of beautiful weeds in an unforgiving forest.

He picked up the quill and dipped it in the ink, fingertips already staining before he'd written a word. He began to sketch the clover, but as he drew, his artistic eye twisted elements here and added a bit there, giving the weed a fresh breath of life. His mind continued to wander along his path, between the failure and success that seemed to ebb and flow like the tide in the oceans he'd read about but had only ever seen from afar. The edges of the clover became a road, and eternal cycle between achievement and disappointment.

When he finished, his clover looked more like four crescent moons intersecting, with nothing concrete to hold them together.

He sighed, and the wave of inspiration that had hit him faded. He stared at the drying ink, feeling as though he were on the cusp of understanding something profound, something that would cement his purpose and equip him to help those who needed him most.

And yet, his muse was gone.

The door creaked behind him, the screech tearing him from his thoughts. The sweet aroma of roses wafted past him, and he smiled. Helen.

"Hi, mischief," he said.

"Hi there, stranger," she answered.

"Did you sleep well?"

She sat beside him and leaned her head on his shoulder. "Like a child. I haven't slept that well in years."

He laughed. "And in an isen's house no less."

She snorted, chuckling along with him. "You're

lucky I adore you. Emmett and I would've ripped a hole in anyone else who tried this."

He held her, his thumb rubbing along her shoulder, and he set his head on hers. "You're right. I'm lucky."

The door slammed open, cracking against the wooden wall with all the force of thunder. Cedric jumped, and Helen flinched beneath his arm. He shifted, twisting around to find Stone at the door, a wild grin on his face.

"I've got it!" the isen shouted.

Helen leaned back just a little, eyes scanning the isen with an expression of confusion with a bit of worry thrown in. "You have what, now?"

"A place for the vagabonds," Cedric said, standing. He offered her a hand and pulled her to her feet. It seemed as though his not-father had come through after all.

"The girl should stay here," Stone said, retreating into the house.

"The girl has a name, you know," Helen said under her breath.

Cedric rubbed her shoulder. "I'm sorry for him. I know he's insufferable."

She shrugged. "I'm not staying, though. I've come this far. I'm not going to wait behind."

"But—"

Emmett stepped onto the porch, grimacing as he passed through the lichgate serving as their front door.

"It seems the old fool has a way for us to protect the vagabonds after all. I suppose we should get this over with as we can be done with him."

"Yes, I'll pack my things," Helen said.

Emmett stood little taller, crossing his arms and blocking the doorway with his bulk. "You're not coming."

"Of course, I'm coming. I fled Hillside, same as you. I'm a vagabond, same as you. In fact, apart from Cedric, I was the first one turned. Besides, there's no guarantee you threw the soldiers in town off our scent. They could track us back here, and I'd be alone. So, let's not play stupid, big brother."

"We have no idea what's waiting for us. The isen only said that it would be dangerous." Emmett shot Cedric a glare, nodding to her as if saying *intervene, please.*

Nope. Cedric shrugged. He wasn't getting in the middle of this one.

Helen gestured toward the forest in exasperation. "What would you prefer? I stay in the isen's house, alone, with some of the most notorious soldiers in Hillside on guard at the bottom of the hill?"

"I dislike both options," Emmett said.

"I don't need to be rescued. I've come this far, and I'm going to finish this journey with you," Helen said.

Emmett groaned and rubbed his face. "Not even Father is this stubborn."

"I'm not asking for permission." She lifted her chin in defiance and slipped between Emmett and the open doorway, disappearing through the lichgate with only the barest of flinches as she passed through the barrier.

The Hillsidian soldier lifted one eyebrow and chuckled, catching Cedric's eye. "She'll be the death of me, I swear."

Cedric laughed and gathered his book and quill. "We have enough enemies as it is, Emmett. Let's not talk like that."

CHAPTER SIXTEEN

AGE 19

Late Autumn

The Cursed Forest

The four of them set off through the woods with nothing more than their packs and a few days' worth of bread and dried meat. Stone led the way, never looking back to so much as check on the party following behind. Throughout their trek, the isen never told them where they were going. Not a hint. Every question was met with silence or a snapped twig.

Cedric and Helen walked side by side, and he did his best to remain patient despite his fading self-restraint. He hated when Stone did this. No answers. No clues. Nothing but silence and an order to follow. It drove him mad. Still, the alternative would be yelling and insults.

Given his choices, Cedric opted for silence.

Emmett, however, did not. "We've been at this for hours, isen, and gone through at least seven lichgates. How much farther?"

"Not far... yakona," Stone added the last word with a twitch of annoyance in his voice.

Emmett cursed under his breath, mumbling something about idiots.

Cedric pushed by a branch and held it aside, so Helen could pass. She smiled as she walked by. Her sweet face numbed his anger, and the quarrel between her brother and his not-father faded into a distant hum. For a moment, he could hear only the beating of his heart.

He and Stone crunched through the forest, twigs breaking beneath their feet even though Emmett and Helen never made a sound. The gift of the Hillsidians— stealth. Cedric envied it. Perhaps when Stone had experimented on him, whatever he had done and removed Cedric's own gift for stealth as well. Perhaps Cedric simply needed more practice, or maybe not all Hillsidians were born with the ability. Regardless, it made travel more difficult.

Stone paused, holding a finger to his lips as he turned toward them for the first time in their trek. He lowered a branch to reveal a wide trail littered with red and orange leaves. A breeze scattered them, kicking them along in small tornados that revealed the occasional square, brick of a cobblestone path hidden beneath. The blood-red path led into a dark forest, the sort of pitch black Cedric only ever seen in the sky. It condensed like a wall, letting no light through, with no hint of what lay beyond.

"We're here," Stone said.

"Well, this looks inviting," Helen said under her breath. Cedric set a hand on her shoulder to comfort her.

Emmett squared his shoulders. "Why did you drag us out here?"

Stone pointed into the darkness. "We'll find an abandoned temple down there. It's a short walk, but the darkness hides it well. Observe."

The isen pushed through the forest and onto the path, leaves skittering beneath his feet. The wind faded like a held breath at his presence. The air grew heavy, thick as a warning. The hairs on Cedric's neck stood on end as Stone lit a fire in his palm, the blaze flickering just above his skin.

The darkness moved.

It shrank away from the fire as if it had a will of its own, as if it had substance. It skirted the flame, not daring to touch it, revealing bits and pieces of what lay beyond the shadows.

Emmett reached his hand around the hilt of the sword at his waist, the creak of his calloused skin across metal the only sound in the quiet forest.

"It's a shadow. I don't think a sword will do much good," Cedric said.

"I didn't get where I am by relaxing," Emmett said. He stepped over a fallen log and joined Stone on the path, somehow avoiding the crunch of leaves beneath his boots.

Helen's soft fingers brushed Cedric's back, and she followed her brother.

Cedric followed suit, the crunch of leaves beneath his boots like a beacon to their location. Emmett shot a glare over his shoulder, but Cedric shrugged. He didn't have their grace.

Each of them lit a fire in their palms to chase away the darkness. Careful and painfully aware of the silence, Cedric kept his eyes trained on the path behind them as they followed the path into the shadows. The darkness engulfed them like water, swallowing the light as they left it until only their flames could guide them on their way through the gloom.

Gradually, the shadows thinned. With each step, the hazy outline of a building appeared in the murky, black fog. It grew clearer with each second, and though Cedric longed to run toward it to escape the darkness, he refrained. Before long, the crumbling ruins of a temple stood before them, a full moon rising over the hazy, blue mountains behind it. Ivy clung to the walls. Moss grew over what was left of the polished steps leading to its door, and a gaping hole in the roof of its leftmost tower revealed fractured rafters rotted with age.

"Good gracious," Helen said under her breath.

"This might work," Emmett said.

Green light glinted off the air beside Cedric. The wisp of green light curved and twisted until a paw popped from it, hovering over the road without a body. Something snapped, like a bone beneath a boot, and a creature the size of a tiger jumped from the shimmying light.

The creature landed on the path, kicking up leaves as it pawed the cobblestone. It was the color of ditch slime—brown with hints of green. Its long teeth curved over its lips and down to its chin. Two, orange eyes glowed with a light of their own, and its tail twitched as it examined them. It growled, the noise vibrating in its throat like a chuckle.

Cedric flinched and stepped back, grabbing Helen and pushing her behind him. Emmett drew his sword, the swish of metal across the sheath like a whistle in the night. The creature however, simply hummed, tilting his head as it watched only Cedric. Its glowing eyes captivated him, almost hypnotizing him with their curiosity.

"*Bloods*, what is that?" Emmett tightened his grip on his sword and stood in front of the party, its blade pointed at the monster.

"Put your sword down, idiot," Stone snapped.

In answer, Emmett shot him a nasty scowl.

Stone rolled his eyes. "By all means, if you'd like to die, engage a lyth in battle."

"A what?" Cedric scrunched his eyebrows in confusion. The name seemed vaguely familiar, but he couldn't figure out why.

"A lyth." The creature's teeth distorted its voice such that it sounded like it spoke with its mouth full.

Helen's mouth dropped open. "It talks."

The lyth's ears flicked back, nearly pinned to its head, and it growled. "It? How rude."

Recollection struck Cedric like lightning. Lyths were rare beasts, loyal to a location and devoted to guarding it until their death. A lyth lived for thousands of years, though, and often served several hundred generations of locations owners. But they were supposed to be myth, creatures that had, perhaps, once lived but long since died out—no one had seen a lyth in eons.

And, more troubling, no one knew what a lyth was capable of.

The creature paced, circling them, its claws grated against the cobblestones with each step. "Rude. Rash.

Loud. Perhaps, I should eat you. After all, I'm so very hungry. It has been many years since anything more than a squirrel walked this path."

Cedric swallowed hard.

Stone gestured to the temple. "I assume you guard this place?"

The lyth nodded. "It has been without a master for many centuries. I've been quite bored."

"We claim it, then. Well, this boy does." Stone pointed to Cedric.

The lyth's cold eyes flicked briefly to Cedric, but it shook its head and sighed with a twinge of annoyance. "The demons have taken over again. They kill and eat, kill and eat. It's all they know, and thus they are no masters to me. Now, you understand why I'm quite bored. If you kill them, you may claim the temple."

"Demons?" Helen asked.

"Disappointing. I assumed the demons were a legend," Stone said.

"You know about this?" Cedric asked.

"Of course."

"And you were going to tell us when, exactly?" Emmett sheathed his sword.

Stone shrugged. "A trivial factor. Now, Cedric, will this suffice as a dangerous area to hide the village?"

Cedric frowned. "Not if there are demons, Stone. Why the hell are there demons?"

The isen groaned with impatience. "The Amber Temple is an ancient place of worship from when a tribe of yakona worshiped a god made of amber. Idiots. And because they were idiots who didn't know what they were doing, one of their rituals opened a portal for the undead. Many claim their actions let in dark things to our world. They tried and failed to close the portal, but they did manage to trap the creatures that came through with an enchanted hourglass."

"Yes," the lyth interrupted. "Many left, but one family remained with the duty of turning the hourglass every year so as to ensure the demons remained trapped and harmless. The last of them died long ago, with no successor. Since his death, the shadow demons have returned, and they have no master. Only the hourglass in the center of the chamber can contain them. As long as the grains of sand within the hour-glass are still, the demons run free within the temple. I keep them contained to the building, but it is all I can do. Enchantments placed on the temple long ago prevent me from going inside."

"That's an odd choice, forbidding the protector from entering," Cedric said.

"They didn't want me involved in their rituals," the lyth said, moonlight glinting off its teeth as it flashed a wicked grin.

A shiver raced down Cedric's spine as he began to

wonder exactly what kind of rituals these so-called priests practiced.

Stone pointed to the temple. "When you turn the hourglass, boy, the demons will be trapped once again. If my source is correct, a lichgate will also appear."

"And you didn't think to mention any of this before he left?" Emmett sheathed his sword.

"Why bother wasting my breath if the place wouldn't work?"

Emmett balled his hand into a fist and frowned, but Helen interrupted him. "So, we have to turn an hourglass? That doesn't sound difficult."

The lyth's tail brushed Cedric's shoulder, and he suppressed a shudder as the coarse fur scratched his skin. The creature chuckled. "Rid the temple of the demons. I will serve whomever turns the hourglass. Do try not to die, for I would hate to have wasted a meal."

The creature jumped into the air, disappearing into a flash of green light.

"Well, he was charming," Helen muttered.

Cedric squared his shoulders and eyed the temple. Crumbling stairs lead the way to a massive set of double doors inlaid with carvings of four-legged monsters with claws and sharp teeth. Shards of glass glittered on the stairs, the marble steps stained with dark spots that reminded him very much of blood. He could only imagine what awaited them beyond the entrance.

"Now or never," he said under his breath.

Back straight, heart in his throat, he walked up the steps with Helen in tow.

Emmett raced up the stairs and stood in front of him. "Stop. Cedric, wait. Have you ever even been in a fight?"

Cedric hesitated. "Well, no. But we don't have a choice, do we?"

The soldier shook his head and gritted his teeth. "Look, you and Helen should just stay out here. I'll handle this."

Helen poked her brother shoulder. "You don't know how many of them there are, Emmett. You could be easily overwhelmed. Don't try to play hero here."

"Unbelievable. They're arguing over who gets to die," Stone mumbled. Cedric shot a glare over his shoulder, but the isen was rubbing his temples in a familiar gesture of annoyance.

Emmett pointed toward the door, apparently oblivious to Stone's comment. "I'm not trying to play hero, Helen. I'm using logic. Neither of you know how to fight, much less defend yourselves. I can't spend the whole time saving you or we'll never get to the hourglass."

"And if you spend the whole time fighting, you may never even see the hourglass," Cedric pointed out.

"But—"

"Let's do this. Together," Cedric interrupted,

worried they were going to talk in circles if he didn't bring up an alternate plan. "I'll go in with you, Emmett, and while you focus on the fight, I'll focus on the hourglass. With the two of us in there, the demons will have to split their attention."

"Ignoring the fact you have no idea what you would do if the demon actually came for you, where's my sister in this plan of yours?"

"Helen waits here with Stone, since I can only assume he won't be fighting," Cedric said, barely able to contain an exasperated sigh.

The isen nodded.

Cedric could barely finished speaking before Emmett and Helen started talking over each other.

"—no! Are you a madman—"

"—I trust you, but not him—"

Stone rolled his eyes and turned his attention onto the empty path. He was likely as bored with this conversation as the lyth was with its centuries of isolation.

"We can't sit here bickering for the next year trying to figure out what to do," Cedric said, exasperated.

Helen set her hands on her hips. "Besides, I do know how to fight. Maybe not as well as you, Emmett, but you and the neighborhood boys would always spar with me when we were kids. I mastered the protection shield. Nothing you shot at me ever hit me."

"Fine! Fine," Emmett said, lifting his hands in a small surrender. "You enter behind me and you stay behind me. Helen, shield the two of you as best you can. And Cedric, look for the hourglass. Try not to be useless."

Cedric grinned. "Useless, now? I have a few tricks up my sleeve, you know."

"Impress me, then." Emmett drew his sword and kicked open the door. It smacked against the walls in a booming echo.

"Subtle." Helen rolled her eyes.

Heart in his throat, time seemed to slow as Cedric drank in the scene before him. Inside, rays of moonlight peeked through a glass dome above, but the light didn't reach the floor or walls. Dozens of columns cast deep shadows through a massive hall. A murky gloom tumbled over the tiles like a dark fog.

A pedestal glowed from its place on a raised platform about a hundred yards away, its body carved from orange amber. A hole had been cut through its center, and even from a distance, Cedric could make out the silhouette of an hourglass in the opening.

"I wasn't expecting this," Emmett whispered as they entered.

The door closed behind them, the click of the latch echoing through the vast space like a thundering reminder of their presence. The echo continued for several minutes, even as they began the long walk toward the pedestal and the hourglass.

The three of them shuffled over the stone blocks of the floor, huddled together beneath the vast archways in the ceiling. The gloom seemed to cling to Cedric's skin like mud he couldn't wipe off, and a dread sank to his toes like weights in his shoes. He shot sidelong glances into the shadows along the edges of the massive room.

A huff billowed from the darkness—a wheezing sigh that made his hair stand on end. A cloud of dust stirred in a moonbeam.

"We should run for it," Emmett said.

Cedric nodded. "Let's get this over with before they come for us."

"On three," Emmett said.

"Three!" Helen said in a harsh whisper. She took off toward the hourglass, and Cedric followed.

They bolted, racing for the hourglass with every ounce of their strength. Despite her head start, Helen trailed behind. Cedric reached a hand toward her, and she took it.

Something screeched. The unholy sound shook the building. Small rocks fell from the arches.

A shadow separated from the darkness behind them, Cedric gaped, his feet slowing as he tried to process what he was seeing.

A demon. The monster was a giant shadow shaped

like an ape. Its edges blurred into the darkness around it, so that there was no telling where it ended or began. The creature towered over him, hunched on its hands. It had no eyes. It roared, revealing the crooked, white daggers that were its teeth. They jutted from every corner of its mouth, piercing its black gums and drawing blood. It snarled and roared again.

Its screech turned Cedric's blood cold.

Three more demons appeared from the gloom-drenched pillars, blocking his view of the pedestal. They bellowed.

Cedric was too late.

The first creature charged, and Cedric focused his attention on his fingers as he summoned his magic. Energy crackled around his skin, hot and sizzling as he reined in its power. He let out a sharp breath, and a bolt of lightning sailed from his fingertips. It hit the demon square in the forehead. A small crater formed in the creature's head, and a trail of smoke curled toward the sky. The beast shrieked, clawing at its face. Yet again, the howl shook the temple. Cedric stumbled. Helen grabbed his arm and pulled him away from the monster. Though her grip barely moved him an inch, he complied as best he could.

A second demon descended on Emmett, its fist the size of the soldier's head, but he sliced at it with the sword. The metal sailed through the demon's arm, severing it. The appendage fell to the ground with a slurping thud. Another scream. Another quake. Dust fell from the ceiling.

Emmett charged the hourglass, his strong legs carrying him toward it faster than Helen or Cedric could keep up. From the darkness, another demon emerged. It swatted at him. He skidded to a stop, kicking up a cloud of dust as he dodged it. Its fists pummeled him, cracking the stone floor each time he rolled out of the way. Face contorted, back arched, he swung at the monster's face. The blade cut through the shadow. A silver gash appeared in the demon's body, and black ooze drizzled from the wound. Its dark goo clung to Emmett's sword, barely dripping off it, but the warrior didn't seem to care.

He turned his intense gaze on Cedric. "Get to the hourglass!"

A blast of green light nearly blinded Cedric as he ran. He fell to the ground, blinking away spots in his vision. Emmett yelled. Helen had disappeared. Cedric spun around, panicking, cursing under his breath, looking wildly around until—

She stood about four feet behind him, hands lifted above her head. A beacon of glowing, blue energy shot from her fingers like a pillar of light. The glow arched overhead, creating a dome of sizzling radiance that stretched about twenty feet in every direction. The dome fell a few feet shy of hourglass.

Yet another demon emerged from the darkness, its

shimmering edges billowing like smoke off a flame. The creature lifted its fists over its head and pounded them hard against the barrier. It shook, popping like corn over a fire.

Helen whimpered. She grimaced, brows furrowed as she struggled with her protection spell. Eyes shut, she huffed. The light emanating from her hands thickened, and a burst of energy crackled along the dome.

Her eyes opened long enough to catch his. Terror shot clear to his toes.

"I'm fine. Go!" she shouted.

"But—"

"I can't hold this forever, Cedric! Go!"

Barely able to breathe, he obliged her. With all his strength, with every ounce of power in his legs, he sprinted toward the hourglass. Dozens of shadowy atrocities emerged from the gloom beyond Helen's dome, one after another. The monsters hammered their fists against the barrier. Screams shook the temple. Rocks fell from the ceiling, sliding along the boundary.

With each blow, the light of Helen's barrier dimmed.

She cried out, a horrible sob of pain that stopped Cedric in his tracks. He slid along the stone, hand falling to the ground as he balanced himself and turned toward her on impulse. She fell to her knees, hands still lifted above her, head bowed almost to the floor.

She wouldn't be able to hold off the giants much longer. The moment her barrier shattered, she would be defenseless.

Every fiber of his being screamed for him to run back, to lift her in his arms and take her with him. Lost to his fear, he scrambled to his feet. If only—

"Cedric! Stop! Focus!" Emmett yelled over the din. The soldier rolled out of the way of a demon's fist headed for his face. The creature's hand cracked against the floor. It yelled, stumbling. A crater remained where its fist had been. Without pausing so much as to breathe, Emmett sank his blade deep into its chest. The beast screamed. The temple trembled, and one of the dozens of columns toppled. The stone support crashed against the floor.

Cedric could save Helen, but only if he reached the hourglass. He hesitated, heart breaking as he watched her double over. Her forehead rested against the stone floor, and she sobbed.

No choice.

He raced toward the hourglass. As he neared, a demon emerged from the foggy shadow clinging to the wall behind it. The monster stood over the hourglass like a mother defending her child, it's white teeth a sharp contrast to its shadow-black body.

He had seconds before he broke through Helen's barrier. Seconds before he faced this thing. He needed a plan, and so far, all he had was panic. He sifted through the hysteria as it drowned out his rational thought, desperate for any of the techniques Stone had taught him over the years, but so far, the only weakness these creatures possessed involved Emmett's sword. He looked over his shoulder, but Emmett sailed through the air, at least thirty feet away.

Too far. He needed another plan.

The lightning had barely affected it before, and even if he had Emmett's blade, he wasn't any good with a sword. He was a scholar, not a fighter.

Still, maybe he would have better luck with fire.

He called his magic to him, and tension pulled on his shoulder blades. Amidst the panic and fear for his and Helen's lives, the weight of the power burning through his core was almost too much to bear. True, he'd felt weaker in Hillside, and stopping at his childhood home had reinvigorated him in ways he had not known were possible. But the strength scorching through his body was foreign even to what he could remember of his abilities as a child.

He grinned, happy to not be useless.

He jumped through the barrier and, just as quickly, let loose a blaze from his fingers. A bonfire rained across the demon, and it screamed in agony. It clawed at its face, its jaws, at every inch the fire touched. The temple swayed. Whole boulders fell to the floor. Several screams echoed together, worsening the quake.

Yet, the massive creature still blocked the hourglass completely.

Out of options, Cedric acted on impulse.

He dropped to the floor and slid beneath its legs, hitting the stairs leading up to the platform with a hearty thud that kicked the air from his body. The demon's legs teetered around him, their wispy edges reminding him almost of the memory he'd stolen from Stone all those months ago.

The creature's knuckle brushed his neck. Ooze clung to his skin. It burned. He seethed, the searing ache so deep he could swear it touched his soul. He couldn't see. Water blurred his vision. His body longed to collapse, to curl in a heap and soothe itself, but he pressed on. With nothing to guide him but his hands feeling along the stone, he crawled up the steps, desperately gasping for air as the temple and monster shook around him.

He reached out, stretching his arm as best he could. His fingers hit the stone pedestal. He inched upward and found cold metal. A hinge. And finally, glass.

The ground shook, worsening until he couldn't tell his own pulse from the vibrations ripping through his body. He could barely breathe. The searing ache worsened on his neck. Thundering footsteps clamored behind him. Someone screamed, and he couldn't tell if it was Helen or the monsters. Metal clanged against stone. Though Cedric desperately wanted to turn around, he knew he couldn't. If he did, he would lose his focus.

If he did, he would lose everything.

He grabbed the top most part of the hourglass and pulled. For a terrifying second, nothing happened. Panicking, he tugged harder. And harder. He pulled with every ounce of strength he possessed, whispering prayers under his breath, bargaining with any divine creature who would listen. He begged and pulled, hoping with all his heart he wouldn't fail. He couldn't. Not now. He was too close.

Finally, the hourglass gave way. It tilted toward him barely an inch and stopped, caught again on something in the hinge. The grains of sand within it shifted.

The rumble stopped. The screaming continued.

Cedric pulled with the last shred of his courage. The hourglass tilted farther, and farther, and farther, until he finally turned it upside-down. Grain by grain, the sand sank into the lower chamber.

Out of breath, Cedric fell to his knees, hands still gripping the hourglass. His vision blurred, and a white light engulfed him. It called him to sleep, promised soothing relief to the ache and terror. His eyes drooped. His head lolled. The faint voice of a woman hummed in his ear like a lullaby, sweet and soft.

Eyes blinking, he fought the song, struggling to stay awake. He had to find Helen and Emmett. He had to know they were okay. If either were hurt, he would never forgive himself.

Never.

"Never," he said to himself as his eyelids drooped. The white light engulfed him. The last of his vision faded. With a sense of relief he didn't understand, and no clue as to what had happened, he fell to the ground.

CHAPTER SEVENTEEN

AGE 19

Late Autumn
The Vagabond's Village

C edric woke to something tapping his cheek. Someone held his shoulders upright. A firm hand held his chin so tightly it pinched, and he pushed it away on impulse.

"Oh, good. You didn't die," a familiar voice said.

Cedric sank to his hands and knees, his body aching. Pebbles and dirt scratched his palms. He tried to open his eyes, but a flash of yellow light blinded him. He cursed under his breath and rubbed his face.

He stared around him, trying to grapple with the blurs of green and brown. Bit by bit, they came into focus. A row of trees. A blanket of grass. Yellow leaves along the forest floor. The forest twittered around him, vibrant and alive. Yet nearby, the branches of two trees crossed in an arch. A lichgate. Through the portal, Cedric caught a diluted glimpse of the hourglass and the Amber Temple guarding it. A column lay in ruins along the edge of the wall.

Stone knelt before him, one elbow on his knee as he studied Cedric's face. "You certainly took long enough."

Cedric shook his head, in no mood for his not-father's nonsense. "Where are Helen and Emmett?"

"Hi stranger," Helen said weakly.

Cedric spun toward the voice to find Helen leaning against a tree, Emmett at her side. A red gash down Emmett's arm had stained his shirt and ripped open his sleeve, but he didn't seem to care. Helen, however, held her shoulder and leaned her head against the tree. Her lips curved in a small smile as their eyes met, but she winced and doubled over, squeezing her eyes shut as creases of pain formed in her brow.

A pang of dread rocked Cedric's core. He ran to her, stumbling in his haste, and knelt at her side. Tenderly, he lifted her hand to reveal a gash. It bubbled, blood spilling over her stained shirt. He peeled back her sleeve to inspect the other side and, much to his terror, blood oozed out the other end as well. She whimpered, gritting her teeth.

"I tried to heal her, but you're better at it," Emmett said without looking away from his sister.

Cedric nodded and set his hand against her wound.

Her blood dripped over his fingers, hot and wet. He didn't care. Clearing his mind as best he could, he channeled everything he had into her wound. All of his energy. His willpower. His panic. His desire. His love for her. Under his breath, he uttered an incantation he'd come up with as a child to help him focus his attention, and though it didn't mean anything, the words had always given a great capacity to heal himself and others.

"Brisbee candor callen trench." He whispered his nonsense again and again under his breath. His hand glowed white, and her shoulder vibrated beneath his touch. Helen gasped and turned her head away, her grip tightening on Emmett's shirt. Her brother didn't flinch, instead pinning her to the tree in an effort to hold her arm still. Cedric's arms burned with the effort of giving forth so much energy, but he didn't stop. He would have given far more to see her safe.

Within seconds, Helen let out a sigh of relief. She relaxed against the tree, and her expression softened. Cedric lifted his bloodstained hand in time to watch the last red edges of the wound close. A scar remained where the wound had been, a shade or two lighter than her skin, but at least she wasn't bleeding anymore.

"Thanks," she said, eyes fluttering closed.

Cedric leaned his forehead against hers, their noses brushing as he finally relaxed, too. "You scared me."

She chuckled. "I had everything under control. Getting hurt was part of the plan."

Emmett and Cedric laughed in unison.

"Are you all quite done? I have things to do," Stone said.

Cedric gritted his teeth, the levity of the moment stolen with the careless comment. Reality sank in. This close call had been too much to bear. Helen could've been seriously hurt, and if Stone had only helped—

With a deep breath, Cedric stopped himself. There wouldn't be any point in starting an argument. Stone would never help. He had his own agenda, his own experiments, his own priorities. Cedric would always be the experiment he entertained, the child he strung along.

He didn't bother bringing any of it up.

"Where are we?" Cedric gestured to the trees to avoid looking at his not-father.

"The eternal forest," a choked voice answered from behind. Cedric twisted around to find the lyth sitting deep in the forest, its tail twitching in the air.

"The what?" Cedric nearly cursed under his breath. Stone and this lyth seem to be perfect for each other— both of them spouted cryptic garbage and expected others to understand what they were talking about.

With another of its unsettling grins, the lyth trotted along the dirt, tail lifted in the air like a cat's. "The eternal forest. This stretch of empty woods goes on forever. But these trees are a mere distraction, meant to disorient those who would attack the temple and who happened to make it this far. The real treasure lies over here, Master Cedric."

Not altogether comfortable with being this creature's master, Cedric offered Helen a hand and lifted her to her feet. Together, they followed the lyth at a much slower pace, Stone and Emmett in tow.

They trudged along for several minutes, Helen leaning on him less and less with each step as she regained her strength. When the lyth finally stopped at a wall of ivy strung between two trees, Cedric's hand on her back seemed to be more for his comfort than hers.

The creature jumped and dug his claws into the vines. As the creature slid to the ground, its claws ripped back the ivy clinging to the short bit of wall in the middle of the forest. But instead of brick or stone, the hole in the ivy revealed a lichgate.

Whereas most lichgates revealed a diluted view of the world on the other side, this one showed only the night sky. Stars glittered like morning dew in the grass. A comet streaked across the dark blue night, leaving an imprint on his vision.

Cedric's lips parted in awe as he stared into the lichgate. He'd never seen anything like it or even read about it in any of the books Helen had brought him over the years. "If we go through, will it shoot us into the sky? Where does this lead?"

"Let us see," the lyth said with a grin. It walked through, the tip of its tail twitching as it passed through this mysterious portal.

"Annoying little bugger," Stone said under his breath. He walked through next without a moment of hesitation.

If Stone had walked through, Cedric had no doubt it would be safe. After all, the isen wasn't prone to endangering himself. Cedric took a deep breath and walked in after them, his hand in Helen's as they entered. Though he expected the typical flare of blue light and a jolt through his body, he experienced neither. Instead of blue light, a kaleidoscope of color broke across his vision; and instead of a kick to the gut, warmth spread through his body, soothing every tired muscle.

Rather than stepping into the night sky, Cedric set foot on grass. He stood in an open field surrounded by trees, with dense forest on all sides. Three white buildings sat in the center of the clearing, their white stone blocks as polished as if they'd recently been built. Despite the state of the temple, there were no ruins here. In fact, Cedric half expected someone to walk out of one of the doors.

"Do people live here?" Emmett asked, apparently having the same thought as Cedric.

The lyth shook its head. "This land is connected to the temple. When the temple's hourglass is still, so is this valley, frozen in time."

"What surrounds it?" Stone asked.

Mountains on all sides, and an ocean to the north. The water goes on forever."

"And how many other lichgates?"

"Two."

Stone nodded. "That will work."

Cedric walked toward the buildings, and the small party followed closely behind. "Why are these three buildings worth protecting?"

The lyth smiled, its wide grin eating most of its face. "Gold is quite worth protecting, so I'm told."

Emmett quirked an eyebrow. "Gold?"

"The temple worshipers were holy men, yet they quite enjoyed things that glimmered. And of course, as the temple is near Ethos, there are many more unclaimed treasures in its ruins" the lyth said. It trotted off and jumped into the air, disappearing in a flash of green light.

"Ethos?" Helen's eyes widened, and she smiled.

Emmett rolled his eyes. "What, the fairytale kingdom where all yakona united in peace? That's a bedtime story."

"I thought so, too. It appears we may have been wrong," Stone said.

Emmett huffed and leaned against the nearest

building, a scowl on his face. Cedric chuckled—apparently the soldier couldn't stand to agree with an isen.

Cedric would ask the lyth about Ethos later. Curious as to what the creature had meant about guarded treasures, Cedric turned the handle on one of the doors. Within, piles of gold coins, plates, and jewelry lay strewn about. His jaw dropped, as did Helen's beside him.

"Oh, my," she said softly.

"Oh, right. The gold. I suppose that will help," Stone said. He crossed his arms and examined the valley.

Emmett leaned in, whispering in Cedric's ear. "He knew about the gold, didn't he?"

"Probably," Cedric muttered.

"He didn't think to mention it?"

"He didn't mention the demons either, if you'll recall."

"He's insane."

"Probably," Cedric repeated. He examined the valley, mind racing with possibilities as he studied the knolls and small hills. There was enough space in the vast field for at least one hundred homes, though he would need to consider land for farming. It could take years to yield any produce, and though it may not happen quickly, their village would need to become as self-sustaining as possible.

Helen slid her hand in his and squeezed. She smiled, and he returned it.

Emmett rubbed his bloodstained neck. "Think this will work?"

Helen nodded. "It's perfect."

"Time to build our home," Cedric said, unable to contain his wild grin.

CHAPTER EIGHTEEN

AGE 22

Early Summer
The Vagabond's Village

I t had taken three years, but Cedric's little village in the valley steadily grew. Emmett had left almost immediately to return in secret to Hillside, to bring his family to their new home. His map had spread through the vagabond network. Each month, one or two new vagabonds would find their way to Cedric. The Hillsidian soldier hadn't been back in years, but word kept trickling back that he was fine, he was recruiting, and he was, one by one, sending his family to the village. Thus far, none of Helen's family had been killed. Many reported mandates from the Blood ordering them to turn Cedric in the moment they saw him, but he grinned with relief each time he heard it. His fellow vagabonds were free men and women now, happily enduring life with the same quirk he'd once thought made him broken.

Cedric leaned back in his chair in his newly constructed study. Each new vagabond brought with them a special gift, from farmers to craftsmen to cooks. Several of the most recent arrivals—three of Helen's cousins—had helped him build a manor in the center of the clearing. His two-story mansion served not only as his home, but also the center of operations for the vagabond cause. The entire first floor contained everything from war rooms to armories and kitchens, but he and Helen had the top floor to themselves. There were also guestrooms for new vagabonds, to give them a place to stay until the home of their own could be built. And one by one, new homes cropped up along the grass, the deep forests framing their little town with a dense thicket of safety.

He sighed with relief, setting his hands behind his head closing his eyes for a moment. The scent of pine, freshly cut from the woods around them, still lingered from the thick desk in his office. One of the new vagabonds had made it for him as a surprise for his birthday, and he couldn't be more grateful.

Well, he probably could show his gratitude by getting back to work. He eyed the paper strewn about his desk—maps and routes Stone had given him before the isen had disappeared again. Cedric hadn't seen

Stone since he'd last gone back to his childhood home over a month ago.

The pendant around his neck dangled as he leaned over one of the maps, the glittering thing catching his eye. He examined it again, the seven-pointed star remained a clunky reminder that he could always go home whenever he wanted. As they had a time or two before in his childhood, he and Stone had changed and locked both of the lichgates in the vagabonds' village to lead directly to his childhood home. Only the key around Cedric's neck could open them, since Stone had insisted he wouldn't have patience for unwanted visitors.

Cedric grinned. His not-father had an odd way of showing his affection, but Cedric would take what he could get.

His eyes shifted again to the maps he had studied a dozen or more times already, half of which he had already memorized. The one in front of him revealed a path through the forests around the Rose Cliffs, a towering cliff face covered with pink blooms where he could gain access to the Kingdom of Kirelm. He wondered what the yakona would look like. He'd heard tales of their wings and silver skin, but it seemed strange to him that yakona could each appear so different from each other.

At any rate, it wouldn't be long before he found out for himself. He hoped as much, anyway.

To succeed, he needed to meet with the Bloods. To date, he had yet to receive an invitation to any Blood's capital. Rumors and speculation burned through the yakona towns as citizens whispered about his powers and abilities. Reed had come to the village with a host of them—apparently, Cedric could read minds, sway hearts with a look, and even breathe fire.

Breathe fire, good gracious. Cedric shook his head. They'd all had a good laugh with that one.

As ridiculous as the rumors became, they suited him. Better to let the Bloods wonder, to overestimate his abilities. To fear him just enough to earn their respect.

You will always be a threat. Stone's reminder floated around in Cedric's mind, and his smile fell.

Over time, he'd sent vagabonds into the outer villages to start rumors about his desire to meet with the Bloods, but he had to otherwise wait for the invitation. The Kirelm capital was somewhere near the Rose Cliffs, and the Lossian capital somewhere near the Villing Caves. Those were his only clues.

With the Bloods at war, Blood Tristan's enemies needed to be Cedric's friends. And Cedric had quite a few to work with. There had once been six kingdoms: Kirelm, Losse, Retrien, Ayavel, the Stele, and Hillside. But the Retrien kingdom had fallen long ago, its bloodline dead, and the Stele had disappeared into the snow with rumors of their Blood's insatiable lust for power.

This left him with four kingdoms to visit, and he certainly wouldn't show his face in Hillside any time soon. For now, he would find ways to visit Kirelm, Losse, and later, Ayavel. When the word came to leave for their capitals, he would be ready.

And yet ...

He groaned and tapped his finger on the paper, slouching in his chair as he lost himself to thought. He had the sense he had forgotten something important, and a heavy sense of foreboding crawled along his shoulders, raising the hair on the back of his neck with a worrisome warning.

In his mind, he again went through the list. He had already copied the maps into his grimoire, so he wouldn't get lost. He'd met with several of his vagabonds who were once Hillside's best guards and soldiers, and they had helped him plan his route. He had debated his strategy with anyone who had an opinion to ensure he hadn't overlooked something in his approach.

Perhaps what worried him most was a rumor that had found its way to him through the vagabonds who trickled into his home: Blood Tristan had labeled him a traitor, to be killed on sight by any Hillsidian who found him or any of the vagabonds he had supposedly turned. Essentially, anyone traveling with Cedric would be killed without trial if they were found by a Hillsidian hunting party.

Cedric tapped his fingers on his desk, frowning. Hillside boasted the best trackers and most cutthroat warriors in all of Ourea. The thought of his own people turning against him in such a violent way sent shivers of dread down his spine.

When he left, at least he wouldn't go alone. He would have some of Hillside's greatest soldiers protecting him.

Thundering footsteps up the stairwell caught his attention. He frowned, leaning back in his chair as the thuds approached his office.

The door swung open, and of all people to enter, it was Emmett. The bulky warrior took up most of the doorframe, his white shirt and broad shoulders blocking Cedric's view of the hallway. Aside from a few creases around Emmett's eyes, he hadn't aged a day in the several years he'd been gone. The soldier waved a piece of paper in his hand. "Have you seen this?"

"It's wonderful to see you, too," Cedric said, grinning.

Emmett smiled and slapped the paper on the desk. "It seems you've arrived, Vagabond."

Cedric lifted the frayed parchment in his hands and scanned the words. A large "V" took up the top third of the page, and beneath it lay a wall of text.

Blood Morden of Kirelm welcomes the Vagabond to his home in the capital. If he so desires, the Vagabond is to arrive at the Rose Cliffs and will be guided from there to the city. He must come alone. Any companions will be killed on sight. Any and all imitators will be executed.

Though a burst of adrenaline and excitement rushed through him at the thought of an invitation to Kirelm, he couldn't help but raise an eyebrow in concern at the last line. "Executed?"

"Of course. Can't have imitators pretending to be you."

"How will he know who I am?"

The soldier rubbed his neck, smile fading. "Word is the Kirelm Blood kidnapped someone who used to work in the castle while you were there. The servant will be able to recognize you."

"That's horrible."

Emmett nodded.

Cedric read the poster again, rubbing his chin as he debated his options. "Where did you find this?"

"Everywhere."

"What?"

Emmett tapped the paper. "I may not respect Blood Morden's propensity to kidnap others, but he's brilliant. These were plastered on every door, every wall, every *tree* in the village I stopped by on the way back. The town was crawling with guards ripping these posters down. But the next morning, every surface was covered yet again. I stayed for three days trying to find out who was behind it but couldn't find anyone, much less a Kirelm."

"Does Blood Morden have Hillsidians working for him?"

Emmett shrugged. "I have no idea."

Cedric ran a hand through his hair, sighing as he leaned back in his seat. "It seems we've been summoned."

"No, you have been summoned. Not me. No one else. You."

"Right," Cedric said. Lovely.

"Of course, you would be an idiot to go alone."

"I agree. The soldiers should still come, but they'll need to stay out of sight on the approach."

"Hillsidians live off the land. We'll be fine while you're in the capital."

Cedric grinned, relieved. "You're coming?"

"Of course. I thrive on eating roots and not taking baths."

They laughed, Cedric rubbing his jaw as he played through scenarios in his head. "But what if Hillside marches to the Rose Cliffs? What's stopping Blood Tristan from—"

"It would be an act of war," Emmett said, cutting him off. "That's why this is brilliant. If Blood Tristan sends an army, they'll be slaughtered. This is Kirelm territory, and they know it better than any Hillsidian. Even those of us going with you need to give the cliffs a wide berth. There will be a long, dangerous stretch where you'll have to go alone."

Cedric squared his shoulders, resolute. "So be it."

Emmett nodded. "I'll get the team ready. We should leave in a few days at the most."

"Agreed."

The door knob turned, and Helen walked in with a smile on her face and a wooden tray of food in her hand. "Hungry?"

"Don't mind if I do," Emmett said. He grabbed the loaf of bread and kissed his sister on the head.

She shook her head but couldn't hide her smile. "Welcome back."

Emmett ruffled her hair and bit into the loaf as he ducked into the hallway. His stomping steps reverberated through the floors.

Cedric reached for Helen as she neared, ignoring the plate. Instead, he kissed her, inhaling the sweet scent of honey and roses.

She chuckled and pulled away, setting one hand on her hip as she gestured to the clutter on his desk. "There's not really place I can put it now, is there? What are you working on?"

"My trip to the kingdoms."

Her smile fell, and his faded as well. She knew the plan. She knew he would leave eventually with no idea of when he would return. The Bloods were demanding, and he would entertain them as best he could.

She frowned. "Do you really think this will work?"

He took the tray of food from her and set it on the maps on his desk, not caring if it stained them. He held her elbows, drawing her close as he kissed her forehead. "The only way we'll get peace is if we ask for it. It will take time, and I don't expect to have a treaty between them on the first visit, but I need to plant the seed in their minds. They don't know what I'm capable of, and at the very least, I'm a curiosity to them. They will see me, and since none of them are particularly fond of Blood Tristan, I have nothing to worry about. They won't turn me over to him."

"But you will be wary? You'll be smart, even if you aren't safe."

"Of course. I'm dashing and clever," he said, winking.

She nudged him, rolling her eyes. "I'm serious."

"As am I. I will come back to you, I promise."

She shook her head. "I want to come."

He sighed and brushed her hair behind her ear. "I know. I love so much about you, but I perhaps love your spirit the most. You're so full of fire, not even Blood Tristan scares you anymore. But you can't. I can't let you come."

She let out an exasperated sigh. "You and Emmett. Where does protecting me end and controlling me begin?"

"Hear me out."

"No! You—"

"Please, Helen."

She paused, arms crossed, lips pursed. She shook her head, eyes squeezed shut. A dimple in her cheek betrayed her nerves—she was likely biting her cheek to keep from crying.

"Please," he said softly.

Her shoulders relaxed. She nodded.

He held her close. "Blood Tristan labeled you a traitor as well as me and Emmett. If you leave the village, you're a target to every roaming Hillsidian soldier in Ourea. If you and I travel together, the other Bloods won't let you join me in the kingdoms. You'll be left behind, every time. And what's worse, they'll be able to confirm that I did in fact change you. They could use you against me. We don't know what will happen, and I don't want you to get hurt."

"But you're taking guards with you for the journey. I'll just stay with them when you leave."

"And if we get attacked on the way?"

"I'll …I'll …" She stared out the window as she trailed off, frowning.

Tenderly, he set his hands on her shoulders. "They can fight, Helen. They've killed before, and they're willing to do it again."

She rubbed her shoulder, the one he'd healed after their run in with the demons in the Amber Temple. For several seconds, she said nothing. Cedric recognized the silence: she must have been debating her options, pausing only long enough to choose her words carefully before she spoke.

"Okay," she said, looking away.

Her quiet agreement wounded him almost as deeply as if she'd yelled. Her disappointment weighed on his chest. He ached to make it right, to make her happy.

He couldn't.

"Be safe, Cedric. I'll wait for you."

He opened his mouth to speak but, at first, he couldn't form the words. He wanted to tell her that she didn't have to. He'd been debating this as well, mulling over his desire and weighing it against her happiness. As much as it pained him to admit, she should love someone else. It would save her the heartache of waiting, constantly left alone without any idea of when he would return, and he had no idea how long he would be. Her happiness meant far more to him than his own. "You don't... you—"

"Hush."

"Helen, I mean it. You deserve a real life, and I can't give you one."

"Nonsense," she said, a small grin spreading over her lips.

"I'm serious."

"So am I," she said, their eyes locking. "I fell in love with the rebel who defied his king, with the kind young man who cared about giving people freedom and choice. I don't know if I could ever love another the way I love you, and quite frankly I don't want to try."

"Even if I'm broken? I don't have a lifeline, I can never bond with you. I don't—"

"I don't care." She kissed him, her soft lips pressed against his. Her rosy scent consumed him, disabling his will to argue.

He hugged her, holding her tight, and the quiet part of him feared it would be the last time he ever held her. He had no idea what awaited him when he left the village, maps or not, and he had no idea how the Bloods would actually receive him. His plan relied on hope and assumptions, not facts, and he hated not having the facts.

As he and Helen stood in his silent office, he savored his final moments with her. Between the fear and panic, he could barely breathe.

True, by all argument, Cedric was a success. He'd escaped Blood Tristan. He'd turned vagabonds of his own, people he could trust. He'd found a village of his own, a safe place among a war-torn Ourea. And yet …

Soon, he would put all of his success to the test and speak to the rulers of Ourea, the royalty that had caused the strife and anguish he was trying so desperately to end.

And once he walked into their throne rooms, he would do it alone.

CHAPTER NINETEEN

AGE 22

Mid-Summer
The Cursed Forest

A fter only a few days of preparation, Cedric
and his team made their way out of the
village.

Twenty of his best soldiers would join him, though
he hoped it was an unnecessary precaution. The
vagabonds cheered him as their group left, and he
shook too many hands to count as he left the manor.
Helen's Father. Her younger brother, Von. Her Uncle
Alder. Her cousin, Aspen. Ronan, one of the guards
from the capital. Hand after hand patted him on the
back. The happy faces blurred together.

Helen walked alongside him, a thin smile on her
face. Her eyes never left him, and each step closer to

the lichgate felt like a betrayal. She slipped her hand in his, and guilt weighed heavily on his heart.

Several of his guards trudged ahead through the portal, but Helen tugged on his hand. He obeyed, facing her. As their eyes locked, the vagabonds' cheers faded to a hum. She swallowed hard, thin smile fading, and pulled him into a kiss. He held her head, heart wrenching at the thought of leaving her.

"Come back, stranger," she whispered.

"I promise, mischief," he said.

With a final goodbye and a forced smile as Helen's father patted his back, Cedric hoisted a bag filled with food on his shoulders and stepped through the starry lichgate that separated the village from the eternal forest outside the Amber Temple. The sword in the sheath around his waist would be basic protection, enough to get him through the forests and to the Rose Cliffs, but it would be useless once he faced the military might of each kingdom he visited. He would have to rely on his wit, which he far preferred anyway.

He trudged through the woods, following the dirt trail his vagabonds had built between the two lichgates. The lyth hadn't been happy with their road, but many vagabonds who entered did so alone, with no idea of where they were going, and he didn't want them to get lost in a never-ending forest.

Thus, the path.

He and his guards travelled in silence for a few

minutes before they found the second lichgate into the temple. Through the archway between two ancient trees, the platform carved from solid amber housed the familiar hourglass in the hole at its center. Grains of sand drifted to a small pile in the hourglass's bottom chamber.

Beyond the platform, the muted darkness of the temple cast a sharp contrast against the bright glow around him. Columns faded away into the depths of the dark shrine.

One by one, they entered. As Cedric walked through the lichgate, blue light flared in his peripheral vision, and a kick to his gut shook him. A chill raced over his body until the hair on his arms stood on end. His shuffling footsteps echoed through the vacant hall, leaving him to wonder if daylight ever touched the place.

He passed the hourglass, the beads of sand falling slowly into the bottom. He tapped it once for good luck and squared his shoulders, trotting down the stairs and past the crumbling column that had fallen in his fight with the demons. The temple was the one thing they hadn't cared to fix—Cedric personally quite enjoyed keeping up the façade of an abandoned temple, despite the brilliant hourglass and the blazing lichgate behind it.

Together, they hustled past the hourglass and down the stairs leading to it, but he couldn't help glancing around. The dozens of columns along the far wall dissolved into a dark haze. He hurried his pace ever so slightly, certain he shouldn't stay in the temple any longer than necessary. Whatever demons the worshipers had invited here were truly evil, and he didn't intend to spend any more time in the vacant hall than necessary.

The temple doors opened as he neared, the iron hinges creaking as the doors came to a stop and beckoned him to the humid air outside. The black haze beyond the temple thinned the air until he struggled to breathe, but he lit a fire in his palm to light the cobblestones and dead leaves beneath his feet.

A flash of green light startled him as the lyth once more jumped into his path. Several of the men cursed, and one drew his sword. Emmett merely rolled his eyes.

"Off on an epic adventure?" The lyth's tail twitched in the air.

Cedric nodded. "You are to continue letting vagabonds in while I'm gone."

"Of course. Who rules in your absence?"

"Helen."

"As you wish. Try not to die."

"Thanks," Cedric said through gritted teeth.

In a flash of green light, the creature disappeared.

"I hate that thing," one of the guards mumbled. Cedric couldn't quite tell who it was—Reed, perhaps.

In the brooding silence outside the temple, Cedric and his team continued along the cobblestones, eager to escape the darkness engulfing the ruins. With each step, the shadow shrank away from his flame. The minutes ticked by, the shroud of darkness gradually thinning until a slim ray of sunshine broke through, glimmering like a sunbeam cutting through murky water. As he stepped from the gloom, a forest surrounded him, the shivering leaves in the canopy above as brilliant green as emeralds thanks to the hot sun shining through them.

Their journey had begun.

C edric's peaceful quiet was short-lived.

With the threat of instant death should a Hillsidian hunting party find them, no one spoke. And after several hours of walking, the silence had become a weight on Cedric's shoulders. The quiet had a presence of its own, a pressure that seemed to watch him, like something hungry hidden in the underbrush. He was used to people, to connection and friendship. And now, he was alone.

It unnerved him.

His stomach rumbled for hours, but Emmett eventually agreed to pause for a bite to eat. The sun blazed overhead, a ticking clock reminding him of his goal to walk eight miles a day. He still had several hours ahead of him before he could find a tree to camp in for the night. A hunger pang twisted in his gut, and he rummaged through his pack before settling on some dried meat and a chunk of bread. He figured he might as well eat the rolls before they became hard as rocks.

The guards fanned out, and before long, Cedric sat alone on a log in the forest. They couldn't be far, but for now, he could appreciate the isolation.

Though he'd expected a break to ease his nerves, the sensation of being watched itched along his neck, stronger now than before. He paused mid-bite to study the forest. The nearby trees barely moved except for the occasional breeze through the canopy, followed by a rush of shivering leaves. A bird twittered as it flew past. A few branches above him shook, kicking leaves to the forest floor as two squirrels skittered by.

Still, he couldn't shake the sensation. He swallowed hard, debating his options.

A twig snapped. He sat upright, eyes darting toward the sound. At first, nothing happened. More twittering. More wind through the leaves. But as the seconds passed, a pair of yellow eyes appeared in the shadow of a nearby bush.

Cedric reached for his sword as a hazy form appeared in the underbrush. A snout appeared. Black fur. Massive paws.

A wolf.

Though Cedric sat on a nearby log, the wolf stood taller than him. He tensed, all but shaking with fear as he gripped the sword hilt at his side. He locked gazes with the creature, each seeming to dare the other to move first. Its glowing eyes were both clear and intelligent, leaving Cedric to wonder if he'd fallen into a trap.

The creature growled. Something about the beast struck him as familiar, but in his panic, he didn't bother to figure out why.

The wolf tensed, and its gaze shifted to the meal in Cedric's hands. His panic ebbed ever so slightly, and he finally caught sight of the ribs evident beneath its thick fur. Its back sloped, its withers too high compared to the painful slope of its spine.

It was starving.

Cedric placed his meal on the ground and nudged it toward the wolf, hoping it would be satiated with his lunch and leave him be. The creature tapped the food with its nose, sniffing deeply, and whimpered. It looked at him again, those brilliant eyes widening as if it were asking him for something he couldn't understand.

It took a few more steps toward him. Cedric flinched, rigid with fear. But as it neared, he finally saw the black rope tied around its muzzle.

His heart broke. Someone had tied off the poor wolf's mouth and left it to starve. If he didn't help the creature, he would never forgive himself. Of course, it might eat him if he did help it.

A conundrum to say the least.

Eventually, Cedric's conscience won over the cold logic Stone had hammered into his brain. He reached for the creature's mouth.

The wolf cringed.

"Shh, it's okay," he said softly.

The creature waited, and after a tense second, it pressed its dry nose into Cedric's hand, the texture like leather along his palm. A flicker of relief shot through him, but he couldn't celebrate yet.

With the tiniest burst of lightning, he cut through the first layer of rope. The wolf whimpered and pulled away, eyes wide. Keeping his voice low and tender, Cedric shushed it yet again and dug his fingers into layer after layer of the black rope. Frayed bits fell to the forest floor until he finally held the last bit in his hand.

The wolf opened its mouth, stretching in a deep yawn as if to test its jaws to see if they still worked. It shook its ragged body, whimpering, and devoured the meal Cedric had left for it in the dirt. It hummed, a noise Cedric didn't think a wolf could make, and looked right at him.

Cedric paused, not altogether certain his act of goodwill had earned him the wolf's good favor. They watched each other, tense and silent as the forest twittered around them.

With one paw in the dirt, the wolf inched toward

him. Cedric stepped backward, ready to bolt if he had to.

Instead of eating him, the wolf licked his arm and then trotted off into the forest.

As it left, the sloping curve of its tail sparked a deep memory. In one of the books Helen had given him during his imprisonment in Hillside—a book whose title he had already forgotten—he'd read a special breed of wolf, the fastest in Ourea. It had black fur, a deep curve to its tail, and a sharp intellect. He wasn't sure if this was the same breed, but it was fascinating nonetheless to think he may have encountered something so rare.

He sat again on his log, his lunch and appetite gone. He reminisced over the encounter, but he couldn't suppress the disgust he felt at the thought of one of his fellow yakona doing something so cruel to an animal, even a predator. He wondered who could even do such a thing.

Perhaps the Bloods weren't the only cruel ones in the yakona kingdoms. Not everything was done at their command—some people simply vented their hatred on the innocent.

Emmett darted onto the path, back arched and sword drawn as he stared after the wolf. He spun, glaring at Cedric. "I can't even leave you alone for two minutes without you getting into trouble."

Cedric shook his head, heart finally settling. "I'm fine."

"'Try not to die.' Did you even listen to that muddy cat of yours?"

Cedric laughed and stood, hoisting the pack on his shoulder. "Let's keep going."

Emmett whistled, and more guards slipped out of the trees and onto the path, some ahead and some behind. Cedric continued along the road beneath the canopy, grateful he'd been able to help the creature. Hopefully, it would stay out of trouble.

As the sun began to set, Cedric's legs ached. He wasn't used to this much activity, even if it was just walking. He longed to sit, to rest, but he had at least another hour before the sun went down, and he had a long trip ahead of him. He couldn't dally.

For the last hour, the canopy had been mostly silent, with a rare bird flying through. Their company marched in silence, Emmett always tilting his head as he studied the landscape. Apart from the occasional scampering animal, the wind bustling through the leaves above was Cedric's only entertainment.

The underbrush shook beside him, and everyone tensed. His hand again rested on the sword at his side, and he watched the bushes, waiting for whatever lurked within to expose itself. The last two times this had happened, bunnies had run out of the bush and across his path, and he'd managed to laugh. But he was a wanted man, a dead man if he was found by the wrong people, and he would take no chances.

A black shadow jumped onto the path and stood beside him—the wolf from earlier. Every one of the guards drew their swords, but Cedric wasn't fast enough. He froze as the wolf watched him, those brilliant eyes honing in on his face. Cedric tensed, taking several slow steps backward.

Cedric shook his hands, loosening himself to run if he had to. Nervous, tired, sore, and not sure what to expect, he waited.

But the wolf sat. Like a dog.

"What on—" Emmett muttered.

The creature tilted its head and pawed at the ground, kicking up tiny clouds of dust. Unsure of what else to do, Cedric continued his walk, careful to keep one eye on the wolf as he left it behind.

The wolf, however, kept his pace. It sniffed the air, ears perked and alert.

Baffled, Cedric paused. The wolf continued for a few steps before stopping as well, its head tilted toward him as it once more sat.

Cedric laughed. "Are you coming with me?"

The wolf whined in answer. Emmett and a few of the other guards laughed.

Cedric continued, and the creature once more trotted along beside him. It must've gone off to eat and come back after it found something more substantial than a few strips of dried meat. As they walked, its rough tongue brushed his arm.

With a grateful smile, Cedric set his hand on the top of its head and scratched its ear. The wolf hummed again, a happy sound, full of warmth and joy. It seemed their adventure had already got off to a most interesting start.

CHAPTER TWENTY

AGE 22

**Early Autumn
The Rose Cliffs**

A cold breeze ruffled Cedric's hair, carrying with it the chill of an ending season. The gust tugged a few leaves off their branches as he hiked through a forest far from his home in the vagabonds' village. The wolf loped along beside him as the sloping hill led them upward, the path winding through the massive trunks of redwood trees on the way to the Rose Cliffs. He was almost there, and dread weighed on his shoulders.

"This is where we leave you, Cedric," Emmett said.

Cedric paused, nodding. "You should look after Ryn."

The wolf at Cedric's side watched him—Cedric liked Ryn as a name for the creature, though he didn't know where it had come from. The wolf didn't whimper or give any indication it had understood, and Cedric didn't quite know what he would do to drive the point home when he reached the cliffs.

"They might try to kill you," he said, a knot forming in his throat. "I doubt they know much about wolves, since their kingdom's in the sky. And they'll hardly let you come. It's not like you can grow wings."

He stopped, and Ryn paused as well. The wolf tilted his head, and Cedric scratched the beast's ear. "You should stay here. I don't know when, but I'll be back. I promise."

Cedric's heart skipped a beat at the promise he wasn't sure he could keep.

The guards slipped into the forest until only Emmett stood on the path. With a sad sigh, Cedric continued down the trail. Ryn followed. He stopped again, lifting a hand to indicate Ryn should stay. Ryn whimpered, and Cedric's heart broke. He scratched the creature's ear again but couldn't help himself. He held the great beasts face and locked eyes with it.

"I'll be back," he said again.

Emmett set a hand on the wolf's head, and Ryn flicked his ears back in acknowledgement. Cedric continued down the path, and this time Ryn stayed in place, whimpering as Cedric disappeared around the corner with a heavy heart and a backpack full of guilt. Ryn could survive on his own, but a part of Cedric worried he would never see the wonderful wolf again.

The forest ended abruptly and opened onto a small clearing overlooking a cliff. Mountains littered the distant horizon, and tiny forests filled the space far below. A gale tore through his hair as he left the protection of the forest, chilling him to the bone. He rubbed his arms and examined the empty cliff face, wondering where the escort was. The poster had simply said to arrive. If he waited long enough, someone was bound to find him.

He wondered how long he would have to wait—and who exactly would find him.

⸙

After an hour of sitting in the middle of the overlook, wind tugging at his hair as he shivered, Cedric retreated to the edge of the forest and bundled himself up as best he could. Often, the bushes nearby would rustle, and a bit of him hoped it was Ryn, safe and out of sight.

The flutter of wings hitting the air eventually caught his attention. He peeked through his bundle of blankets and his one good coat to find several figures sailing through the air, nothing but silver blurs as they sped toward him. He pushed himself to his feet, panic blasting through him.

It seemed his envoy had arrived.

A great creature flew behind them with a saddle on its back—a griffin. Half eagle, half lion. He caught glimpses of the silver feathers along its neck, the sharp orange beak, the talons. Its feathers faded to black fur along its back, and its lion tail whipped behind it as it kept pace with his guides. He'd read about griffins, about how Kirelm prized them as the best mounts in the world. Given his lack of wings, he could only assume this one was met for him.

He grinned, excited despite his anxiety.

The soldiers landed, four of them. Their silver skin glistened in the sunlight like soft metal, but the hardened expressions on their faces gave them the look of warriors. Like Emmett. With a pang of remorse, Cedric wondered when he would see his friend again.

If he would see his friend again.

He cleared his throat to shake the thought from his mind and bowed in welcome to his guides. They were taller than him, and their wings stretched beside them to fill as much space as possible. Three of them had gray wings, one black.

The soldier with black wings walked toward him. "Your name?"

"Cedric, the Vagabond. I have a meeting with—"

"We know. Here," the soldier interrupted, grabbing

the griffin's reins from one of the other soldiers and handing them to Cedric.

"Thank—"

"Let's not waste time." The soldier took off into the air. The gust from his takeoff ruffled Cedric's clothes, and he shielded his eyes from the biting sting of the wind. The other guards joined him. They flew away, though at a slower pace than before, and Cedric took the hint. He gathered his things with the reins drooping from one hand, stuffing his blankets in his bag as fast as he could.

"I'll be back, Ryn," he whispered to the silent underbrush.

The griffin cooed, tilting its head as it watched him. Hesitant, not entirely sure how to handle a griffin, Cedric patted its neck. It squawked loudly, the sound nearly shattering Cedric's ear, and he flinched. His ear rang, and he rubbed it, grumbling.

Carefully, tenderly, he inched around the creature and tried his best to jump on its back. He slid off twice, face reddening with frustration each time, until the griffin finally knelt for him. Relieved and embarrassed, he hopped on and nudged it gently with his heels.

The griffin took off as if he'd slapped it.

Forgoing the reins entirely, he wrapped his arms around its neck and suppress the urge to yell as the creature dove off the edge of the cliff and spread its giant wings. He squeezed his eyes shut, stomach twisting as the ground disappeared. It took every ounce of his willpower not to scream.

The griffin banked to the right, and Cedric's grip around its neck tightened. He hoped he was important enough to catch if he fell, but he didn't want to bet on it. As the griffin caught up to the other soldiers, he caught a few of their chuckles over the howling wind. He didn't care. He was entirely focused on not falling to his death.

§

Roughly an hour later, Cedric stood outside the closed throne room door, waiting to be told he could enter. He wiped his sweaty palm on his new pants, grateful for the bath they'd forced on him. He'd been informed by a young lady who greeted him at the steps that, with his filthy clothes and face stained with his nights spent outside, he was in no condition to meet royalty. He was promptly escorted to a room and given access to more bath salts and soaps than he had ever seen in his life, which he quite enjoyed considering the weeks he'd spent outside. The girl had grimaced upon meeting him, so he wondered how badly he had smelled.

Without warning, the throne room doors opened onto a massive hall lined with soldiers. Three thrones sat on the platform at the far end, though only two were filled. A tall Kirelm wearing a thick, silver crown sat in the center chair, his white wings curled behind him. A younger Kirelm sat to his right, his crown and face almost identical, if younger.

The Blood and his son, no doubt. Though the third chair—it sat empty.

Cedric entered, back as straight as he could muster, knees trembling, chin held high. He had to portray confidence, even if the Blood's presence reminded Cedric of being brought before Blood Tristan in chains.

"Thank you for having me, Blood Morden," he said to the man in the center throne.

The Blood leaned his elbow on his arm rest and rubbed his chin, studying Cedric without speaking a word. Cedric's footsteps echoing through the massive hallway was the only sound, despite the sheer volume of soldiers along every wall. No one coughed. No one sneezed. Not a single piece of fabric rustled. They somehow stood in utter silence, nothing but breathing statues flanking Cedric's seemingly endless walk to the thrones. He suppressed the impulse to fill the silence with mindless chatter. Each soldier he passed look straight ahead, no one but the Blood and his son acknowledging him.

Cedric wanted to squirm, to gulp and maybe even back up slowly, to assure the Blood this was unneces- sary, to go back to his village, to come up with another idea. But he had come this far, and he wouldn't quit because of an imposing welcome. He'd known the risks —they could turn on him at any moment, and only the promise of the next visit kept him safe. He had to convey power and authority, even when he felt small.

He was, after all, the Vagabond. People looked up to him. Bloods feared him. He had made promises to his vagabonds. They expected things of him, and he would deliver.

"Prove to me you are who you say you are," the Blood said, his voice booming.

A jolt of panic shot through Cedric's chest as he remembered the Hillsidian servant Blood Morden had supposedly kidnapped. "As I understand it, you have someone who can do that for me."

The Blood smirked, eyes narrowing. "It seems you have better spies than I realized. Of course, so do I."

The dread returned to Cedric's chest like a rock pressing down on him and suffocating his body. He knew the Bloods had their means of getting information, but he'd never considered spies following his vagabonds, knowing who they were. It compromised everything. "And what have your spies told you?"

"Enough. For instance, you locked the lichgates into the Hillsidian capital. In the past, I was able to send spies into the Hillsidian capital itself, and yet when I tried to post my notices for you there, we were unable to enter. I admit, I'm impressed with you, Vagabond."

Cedric nodded his head in thanks. "What else have you learned about me?"

The Blood clicked his tongue. "That's not your concern. Now tell me, Vagabond, why you are here."

"For now, I simply wanted to meet you."

The Blood grimaced, the expression an odd mix of confusion and annoyance. "You possess the skills to lock lichgates, have the power to disobey your Blood, and yet you simply wanted to speak with me?"

Cedric paused, gathering his thoughts before he spoke. He needed to tread carefully. "In time, I want a ceasefire between the kingdoms. Peace. No more war. For now, yes, meeting you will do."

The Blood waved his hand in the air, motioning for Cedric to hurry up. "No, tell me why you are really here. You want allies against Blood Tristan? An onslaught against the Hillsidian capital? I happen to know you have an army of your own, and I can only imagine what for."

For a moment, Cedric couldn't speak. The Blood knew too much. It terrified him. It could mean the village was compromised or—

No. No, he needed to focus. He needed to stay present, aware of his surroundings. Eventually, he forced himself to say something—anything—to hide his horror. "No, my Blood. Only peace."

Blood Morden studied him like an insect, as though he would squirm beneath a king's glare if it held long enough. The Blood's lips parted ever so slightly in what Cedric could only assume was disbelief. "Don't lie to me, boy."

Cedric shook his head. "I'm not. True, Blood Tristan is cruel. Yes, he mistreats his subjects, commanding and controlling them in ways no ruler should. Yes, he was the motivation behind my movement and showed me what is wrong with this world. But I have no intention to attack him. I want only peace."

"Yakona have never known peace."

"They have, long ago. In Ethos."

The Blood rubbed his forehead, exasperated. "That's a fairytale."

"It was real. I read forbidden books from the Hillsidian library, researched it myself. I've spoke to a lyth who lives in the ruins. It was possible once, and it can happen again."

The Blood quirked an eyebrow but didn't answer. In fact, he simply watched Cedric, no doubt debating options Cedric didn't want to think about. He didn't seem to be entertaining Cedric's request, despite what he had written so long ago. Despite what he thought they had already begun to discuss in their letters. Nervous, anxious, it was all he could do to stand still and maintain the Blood's eye contact.

"You're welcome to stay, Vagabond. Perhaps we can discuss your," he hesitated, barely able to suppress a sneer, "peace negotiations in more detail."

Cedric swallowed hard, his palms clammy as he lost the final shred of control over the conversation. The Blood stood, their meeting apparently over. And with that, a guard grabbed Cedric's shoulder and ushered him out of the room.

CHAPTER TWENTY-ONE

AGE 22

Later that day
The Rose Cliffs

As the sun set, Cedric walked around the palace grounds with his hands in his pockets. One of the guards had informed him he was permitted to roam the castle, but everywhere he went, eyes followed him. He swore even the eyes in a painting had tracked his movement through a hall. The tickle on the back of his neck never ceased unless he was in the room they had given him, and even then, he doubted he could speak with freedom.

He kicked a pebble, wondering what the hell he'd got himself into.

With a deep breath, he closed his eyes and stepped into a beam of sunlight, savoring its warm kiss on his skin. He couldn't give up—he wouldn't. He refused. Staying was not a failure, just a setback. He was asking for something that had not been achieved in millennia, something many believed was nothing more than a myth: an Ourea in which no one fought, in which the yakona were allies. With time, they would listen. With time, they would change. And Cedric would never stop.

A cloud passed between him and the sun, casting a cold shadow over him. A flicker of doubt bloomed within him, and it was all he could do to silence it.

"Look out!" someone yelled.

Cedric jumped, snapping to attention. Men clambered, hollering in the distance. He ran toward the ruckus, rounding the castle until he saw a group of soldiers circling a massive griffin, easily twice Cedric's size. It reared, its talons kicking at the air. The beast stretched its great wings, blocking out a sliver of the sun.

"It's escaped again!" a man shouted.

Voices clambered over each other.

"—the rope—"

"—great, stupid thing—"

"—it bit me—"

The creature broke through and charged into the field, screeching as though it had a knife embedded in its hide. It ran for its life, feet thundering over the grassy field. Cedric froze, wondering what to do—

should he attack it? Immobilize it? For the moment, he simply watched as it ran, wind ruffling its white feathers. It closed its eyes as it galloped through the grass, lifting its beak as if to savor the fresh air.

Cedric relaxed his shoulders. It just wanted a bit of freedom. He could relate.

It bucked at the air, the motion shifting its path. It circled, racing ahead, this time directly for Cedric. It caught his eye, and the creature's body language shifted. It tucked its wings in close. Shoulders tense. Head down. It focused on him, never letting him out of its sight as it charged.

Cedric tensed, arching his back as he steeled himself. He hadn't dealt much with charging animals, but he had taken on shadow demons and defied kings. In some of his books, he'd read about charging griffins. The territorial creatures looked for fear, exploited it. To survive a griffin charge, he needed to hold his ground.

He cracked his knuckles, willing himself enough nerve to persevere despite the instinct to run. He balled his hands into fists, hoping he was doing the right thing. To be safe, he hid one hand behind his back, summoning fire into his palm should he need to deter the beast from attacking him.

The animal charged. He held his ground.

Twenty feet remained between them.

It lowered its head almost to the grass.

Fifteen feet.

Cedric sucked in a deep breath, tensing as he prepared to unleash the fire that would no doubt slow it down.

Ten feet.

The animal skidded, digging its front feet into the ground, kicking up clumps of dirt. The griffin slid along the grass, pulling it up by the roots, and only stopped when it was nearly nose to nose with him. It paused, breathing heavily, as it stared him down.

Its eyes dilated as it studied him, sharp and intelligent. For a piercing moment, it seemed almost as though Cedric were looking at Ryn once more. The great wolf had offered him companionship and aid when he needed them most. All it had ever asked in return was kindness.

Perhaps this griffin wanted the same.

Fingers shaking ever so slightly, Cedric lifted his left hand tenderly, carefully, as his right remained hidden and filled with fire so that he could use his flame should the need arise. He reached for the griffin's face. It shied away as he neared, eyes shifting between his rising hand to his face, but he slowly inched toward the feathers along its beak. A low growl rumbled from its throat, but he kept eye contact and continued.

Every second ticked by, each more painfully slow than the last, but he finally set his hand on its cold feathers.

Its eyes snapped to him, and it relaxed ever so slightly. It didn't budge. Inspired by the fact it hadn't killed him yet, Cedric rubbed his thumb along its beak, the cold feathers like silk beneath his touch. The griffin cooed, leaning into his hand, and closed its eyes.

Cedric smiled and extinguished the fire hidden behind his back.

"It seems you're full of surprises, Vagabond," a familiar voice said.

Careful not to surprise the creature inches from his face, Cedric peeked out of the corner of his eye to find Blood Morden nearby. The griffin growled again, the low rumble similar to distant thunder, and nipped the air in the Blood's direction. It squawked, as if warning the Blood to stay away.

"I just wanted to help," Cedric said with a smile, happy to have calmed down something as intimidating as the griffin. This was sure to impress the Blood— after all, none of his soldiers had managed. Cedric ran his hand along its face again, and the creature cooed once more.

"That is my royal griffin, Vagabond, only I and the griffin handlers are to touch it. It's a prize steed, one meant only for royalty. Yet you insult me by stroking it as if it were a dog?"

Cedric's smile fell, and he stepped away on impulse. The griffin followed him, pushing its head against his chest, asking for more attention. "I apologize, Blood Morden. I had no idea—"

"Enough." The Blood grimaced at the creature and glared at Cedric with equal disdain before turning on his heel and stomping away. Cedric groaned, and dread sent ribbons of ice through his veins. The griffin clucked softly, tapping its sharp beak on his shoulder. He flinched in pain, but the creature rubbed its head against him again.

It seemed in his attempt to win over the Blood, Cedric had failed once more.

After leading the griffin back to its stall—since it lunged at anyone else who tried to lead it away, including the Blood's son—Cedric leaned against the window pane in a tower high in the castle. He suspected there was still a guard somewhere that kept tabs on him, but he didn't care. From here, he could see the whole kingdom, and he leaned his head against the cold stone as he studied its buildings, frustrated. He needed to get back in the king's good graces, and he didn't have the faintest idea of how to do it.

The gentle patter of footsteps in the stairwell to find him caught his attention. He didn't budge, instead watching the stairwell out of the corner of his eye as he waited for one of the soldiers to no doubt tell him to leave.

Instead, a beautiful Kirelm woman round the corner. Her glimmering wings and flawless face gave her the appearance of a walking, breathing statue made of polished silver. She smiled as she caught his eye, and only then did he notice the thin, blue crown on top of her head.

He bowed abruptly. A crown meant royalty, and though he had no idea who she was, he needed to respect the royal family. Especially here.

She laughed. "No need for such formalities. No one knows I'm here."

He hesitated, eying her cautiously. "Why is that?"

"Because I'm about to discuss something my husband despises."

"You—you're—"

"I'm Queen Louise, yes. I read through the letters you've sent us, though I should hope you don't tell anyone. Women in Kirelm aren't meant to meddle in politics."

"Your secret's safe with me."

She smiled. "I know. Though Blood Morden disagrees, I think peace in Ourea would bring about an age of prosperity. Wealth. Safety. Advancement. I see no reason to squabble as we do. I think yours is an honorable goal, if not a necessity we should all strive for. We don't have much time to talk now, but I wanted you to know you have at least one friend here in Kirelm."

He nodded, about to thank her, but she spun on her dainty heels and left without another word. He almost told her to wait, but thankfully squashed the impulse. He knew better than to command royalty. As her footsteps faded, the second flicker of doubt that day burned in his chest.

Cedric needed friends. He needed connections. But a part of him didn't believe her. After his reception with the Blood, he wondered if the Queen could truly be so different—or if this was all a trick.

CHAPTER TWENTY-TWO

AGE 22

Mid-Autumn
The Kingdom of Kirelm

I n the weeks following his meeting with Blood Morden, Cedric received less and less attention from the royal family. Queen Louise came to speak to him several times in the tower, but their meetings were always cut short and nothing much came of them. She asked once how she could help, and Cedric admittedly had no idea. Aside from convincing the Blood to join his cause, which she admitted she could not yet do, Cedric didn't feel like there was anything to be done.

At least, nothing he trusted her with. Not yet.

Cedric sat on the floor by his bed, staring at the wall

with the only window in it. He leaned his head against the mattress, watching the endless sky above. He'd lost track of how long he'd been sitting in this position as the stars rotated overhead. Eventually, his stomach rumbled.

He should've met with the Blood today, but the meeting had yet again been canceled. It had become a worrisome habit of the Blood's to disappear, to become unavailable when they had agreed to discuss Cedric's purpose for coming to the Kirelm capital. The day stretched on, and Cedric wondered how much longer he could stay without losing the Blood's respect. How much longer he *should* stay before calling it quits—at least for the time being.

In all likelihood, the Blood had no interest in discussing any of the terms of the treaty. Cedric was a threat, as Stone had pointed out all those years ago. He had no blood loyalty, and the circulating rumors that he could change others had filled even the castle. The looks he got now were different than the leery distrust he'd encountered at first. Now, more servants nodded to him as he passed. Some even smiled. Some hesitated, shoulders tense, and he wondered what they wished they could say.

There were more rumors, outright lies about what he could do, about his power. Some said he could kill with a touch. Others insisted he was the most powerful yakona alive, stronger even than the Bloods. And though the rumors were rubbish, he began to appreciate them. He wondered, now, if those rumors were the only reason he was still alive.

He was a threat, and he was being kept where the Blood of Kirelm could keep an eye on him.

Cedric's mind wandered back to home to his village, to Helen. He relaxed, and with the memory of her beautiful face managed to suppress his frustration ever so slightly. Failure was no option for him. In the beginning of any task, there would be challenges. He had to prove how badly he wanted this. It would be harder than he ever thought possible to unite the kingdoms, and this roadblock in Kirelm was nothing more than a test to see if he was truly dedicated.

He was. He would see this through to the bitter end.

Cedric stood, making up his mind and stretching as he looked out onto the sky. Next came Losse, a kingdom entirely underwater. Regardless of whatever Blood Morden told him in their next meeting, Cedric would leave for Losse in five weeks. He would stay in each kingdom for, at most, two months, always moving on, traveling from kingdom to kingdom until he had news, something to bring home. And he would, with time. With Kirelm, Losse, and Ayavel finally on his side, he would have the support to finally talk some sense into Blood Tristan.

Cedric smiled, a sliver of hope replacing his doubt. In his heart, he knew this would work—even though all the evidence and all his experience thus far pointed to the contrary.

He simply had no other choice.

IMPORTANT CHARACTERS AND TERMS

๕๑

MAIN CHARACTERS

Kara Magari - Born in our world but dragged into Ourea by fate, Kara Magari was raised a human but soon finds out she's much more as she becomes the second Vagabond and master of the powerful Grimoire.

Braeden Drakonin - A Stelian Heir raised as a Hillsidian orphan, Braeden loathes his heritage and rejects his lineage. When he meets Kara he thinks he's found a way to officially leave behind his past and start a fresh life free from his cruel father.

꧁

OTHER CHARACTERS BY KINGDOM

HILLSIDE

The Hillsidian race is most similar to humans in appearance. Hillsidian blood is green.

Notable Hillsidian Characters:

Gavin - Heir of Hillside. Cunning, aggressive, and a bit of a womanizer. Raised as Braeden's brother.

Richard - King to the Blood Lorraine, ruler of Hillside and Gavin's mother. He and Gavin don't have much of a relationship.

Twin - A palace servant and close friend to Kara Magari.

Blood Lorraine - Ruler of Hillside. Mother to Gavin and adoptive mother of Braeden.

AYAVEL

The Ayavelian race is characterized by the triple irises in their eyes.

Notable Ayavelian Characters:

Blood Aislynn - Blood of Ayavel. She has spent her life brokering peace between the kingdoms and has, to some degree, succeeded. She has no children or Heirs of her own.

Evelyn - Blood Aislynn's niece and chosen ruler of Ayavel upon her aunt's death.

KIRELM

Kirelm people live high above the ground in a kingdom that floats over the Rose Cliffs and therefore have wings to travel.

Notable Kirelm Characters:

Aurora - Daughter to Blood Ithone and Heir to the kingdom, though she is the first female Heir in their kingdom's history. Their culture celebrates men as the leaders of the race, rather than women, and this has been a great shame to her father.

Blood Ithone - Ruler of Kirelm. Set in the ways of his culture, he has always been disappointed that he did not have a son to call his heir.

STELE

Stelians have grey skin and smoke steaming from their pores. They can change form to mimic other yakona races.

Notable Stelian Characters:

Blood Carden - A cruel ruler with a vendetta against the other kingdoms. He has worked tirelessly his entire life to get revenge, and he's so very, very close.

Queen Myra - Blood Carden's murdered wife and Braeden's mother. There's more to her death than meets the eye, and Braeden is determined to get his revenge.

LOSSE

Lossians can breathe under water which comes in handy since the kingdom of Losse is beneath the sea in a protective bubble.

Notable Lossian Characters:

Blood Frine - The careful, cunning, and manipulative ruler of Losse. He prefers to keep to his isolated kingdom and let the other kingdoms war with each other.

ISEN

Isen are soul stealers. By stealing a soul every decade or so they can stay young forever, but at a cost: the more souls they possess within them, the more likely they are to lose their minds. Isen can take the form of the souls they steal and impersonate their victims. A small retractable barb in their wrist is inserted into the neck of their victims in order to capture their soul.

Notable Isen Characters:
    Deidre
    Niccoli
    Agneon

DRENOWITH

The Drenowith are also known as muses. These immortal creatures are very difficult to kill and have the ability to take the form of any creature, but they cannot reproduce. It's said they've been around since the first days of the Earth and prefer to be left to their own devices. Their magic is the cause of many, if not most natural disasters.

Notable Drenowith Characters:
　　Adele
　　Garrett
　　Verum
　　Mirrow

⚶

KINGDOMS AND NOTABLE PLACES OF OUREA

Hillside - A beautiful maze of trees. The castle itself isn't made from stone or dead wood, but is rather comprised of the five largest trees in the kingdom, all of which sit in the middle of the sprawling city. Those who live and work in the castle use the hundreds of rope bridges to cross between the rooms hollowed out of the trunks. It's a green paradise and a kingdom ruled by the Hillsidian Blood. Brilliant walkways span out from the castle like rays on a sun, the paths covered in shifting stones that take the shape of whatever touches them.

Ayavel - A kingdom of light ruled by the Ayavelian Blood. Ayavelians have the rare ability to shapeshift into any of the other yakona, as long as they practice early in life. Their natural skin is iridescent, glimmering like diamonds, and they possess eyes with three irises in them that can each convey subtly different emotions. The Kingdom of Ayavel is surrounded by a tall, white wall that protects the kingdom. The city is comprised mainly of white buildings trimmed with gold that have domed roofs and towering golden spires. The roads are lined with cherry blossom trees and their petals fly through the air with the breeze.

Kirelm - In the clouds somewhere near the Rose Cliffs of Ourea, the kingdom of Kirelm floats above the surface. Two layers of intricate and impenetrable wires keep intruders out while allowing the sunlight in. The silver-skinned people of this kingdom are equipped with massive wings in shades of white, gray, and black which allow them to travel throughout this kingdom in the sky ruled by the Kirelm Blood.

The Stele - A dark and dangerous place, the Stele is a

home to many of Ourea's most terrifying creatures. Long ago banished from the other yakona realms, the Stelians are a culture of outcasts who resent their centuries of banishment. Like the Ayavelians, Stelians possess the ability to shape-shift, but their true form is the stuff of nightmares. Their ash-gray skin spews smoke when they're angry, and there are no whites to their eyes. The Stelian Blood rules over this kingdom.

Losse - This underwater kingdom is only accessible to those who can breathe underwater or those who are able to take the sting of the magical starfish that temporarily filters air from the water long enough to reach the kingdom's gate. Once in the protective golden bubble that encompasses the kingdom with air, the starfish is no longer needed . . . unless you want to leave, that is. Lossians have blue skin and large seaweed-green eyes. Most of them are bald, but some have black hair. Their thin form and webbed feet help them swim to their kingdom while breathing under-water. The Lossian Blood is the ruler of this kingdom.

The Villing Caves - Once a celebrated haven of caverns and lakes, the Villing Caves became the resting place for the Retriens. The long-lost yakona kingdom had claimed this place as their own after the fall of Ethos, but a dragon invasion soon thinned them out. In a last-ditch effort to protect his people, the Retrien Blood had no choice but to seal himself and the dragons into the caves. However, his Heir did not awaken as the new Blood, and so it's believed that the Blood still lives trapped inside the stone.

The Vagabond's Village - The Vagabond's Village is where the first vagabond and his followers lived. The Vagabond himself lived in a lavish mansion surrounded by the beautiful stone cottages his followers lived in, all of which was safely tucked away in a wooded valley. There is only one way to enter. First, visitors must get past the Lyth before attempting to pass through the terrifying Amber Temple, a place of worship which long ago opened a portal to deadly demons that took over the surrounding area. These creatures can only be contained by a glowing magical hourglass, but be warned: if the sands within are moving, the demons are trapped; but as soon as the last grain falls, they are free again.

Ethos - The abandoned city of Ethos is where all the yakona races once lived in unity and peace. There is little facts still known about its fall, but it's said the Stelians were at fault and that is, at least in part, the cause for their banishment. It was the First Vagabond's goal to reunite the kingdoms once more and rebuild Ethos.

❧

GLOSSARY

Yakona - The yakona are one of the peoples of Ourea and known to be true masters of magic. Over eons, the six races have evolved to look quite different from each other: the Ayavelians, the Stelians, the Hillsidians, the Kirelms, the Lossians, and the Retrien.

Bloods and Heirs - Bloods are the rulers of each yakona kingdom, given the right to rule by unique magic in their blood that's passed from parent to child. The Bloods are connected to their subjects through a shared blood connection, which allows them to control the actions of their people via mandates and blood-bound orders. Heirs possess a lesser version of the blood magic, though Bloods and Heirs heal almost instantly from a wound. Upon a Blood's death, the Heir awakens and takes on the powers of his or her predecessor. The awakening is an incredibly painful process, thought to be the most painful experience known.

Sartori - Sword belonging to the Blood of each race. Only the Blood can wield the sword as touching the hilt will burn anyone else. The entire blade is coated with the only known poison that can kill a Blood, and each Sartori has a slight variation of the poison. An antidote can be made, but only from the blade that caused the wound.

The Grimoire - The First Vagabond created the Grimoire to document everything he knew about Ourea so that it could be passed down. The magical book can flip its own pages, make drawings come to life, and so much more.

The Vagabond's Necklace - The four-leaf clover pendant has a stone in the middle. It's able to hide the Grimoire from sight so that those who seek the power within cannot steal it. The stone can be clear, which means the Grimoire isn't magically hiding within the stone, or blue, which means it is. Only the Vagabond can call the book forward or wish it away.

Blood Loyalty - Each kingdom has a ruler called a Blood. The Blood can control the people in their kingdom through the blood loyalty. Anyone given a silent or spoken command must follow it. Cedric, the First Vagabond, discovers that he does not have a blood loyalty, and therefore does not need to follow commands given by his blood.

Lichgates - A lichgate is a portal that ties our world to the terrifying and beautiful world of Ourea. Lichgates can be found in remote places, and when you walk through a lichgate, the land you cross into is not what you would see if you'd simply walked around the portal. There are also lichgates within Ourea that can make traveling vast distances easier... if you know where they are.

Ethos - Ethos is an ancient city which once housed all the races of Ourea in one place. They lived in harmony until it was discovered that a Stelian figured out a way to steal the bloodline from other yakona royal families. After that, Stelians were banished and trust between the yakona races eroded. They all went their separate ways and abandoned Ethos.

YOU'RE MISSING OUT...

Boyce posts official artwork, updates, and random things that will make you laugh on Facebook, Instagram, and Twitter.

Boyce also created a special Facebook group specifically for readers like you to come together and share their lives and interests, especially regarding the Grimoire Saga novels. Please check it out and join in whenever you get the chance! Everyone in there is amazing, and you'll fit right in.

https://www.facebook.com/groups/Grimoire-Readers/

Sign up for email alerts of new releases AND exclusive access to the Grimoire Saga Fandom Encyclopedia: the official guide to Ourea exclusively for the Grimoire Saga's biggest fans. The encyclopedia is

ONLY available to Boyce's VIP email tribe, so sign up now to get access:

https://smboyce.com/email-signup-pages/grimoire-saga/

Enjoying the series? Awesome! Help others discover the Grimoire Saga by leaving a review at Amazon: **http://mybook.to/first-vagabond**

BOOKS BY S. M. BOYCE

The Grimoire Saga

Lichgates

Treason

Heritage

Illusion

The Misanthrope

The First Vagabond: Rise of a Hero

The First Vagabond: Fall of a Legend

The Demon

The Fairhaven Chronicles

Glow

Shimmer

Ember

Nightfall

Standalone Novels

Ari

ACKNOWLEDGMENTS

My amazing beta readers helped shape this novel, so special thanks to Dad and Rob Zimmermann. And of course, my content editor/husband is an epic badass who let me bounce ideas off him instead of having quiet dinners like normal people. Thank you, Geoff.

ABOUT THE AUTHOR

S. M. Boyce is a lifelong writer with a knack for finding adventure and magic. Known for enchanting, expansive, and epic worlds, Boyce writes action-packed adventures with heroes who push boundaries to make their worlds better.

Word-of-mouth is crucial for any author to succeed. If you enjoyed this novel, please consider leaving a review at Amazon, even if it's only a line or two. Your review will make all the difference and is hugely appreciated.